MYSTIC PERCEPTIONS

Book I

Mystic Gifts Trilogy

BY

Jacqueline Paige

Published by FRP
Copyright © 2021 Roxane Kerr
Edited by Gaele L. Hince
Cover art by: Off the Wall Creations

Previous edition released in 2010

Excerpts from *Café Serenity* by Jacqueline Paige, *Heart* by Jacqueline Paige and *The Huntress* by J. Risk copyright ©2014, 2105, 2017 by Roxane Kerr

ISBN: 978-1-990763-25-0

Sandy smirked as the men moved to sit. "I'm warning you, the first obscenity or foul name you use, I'll have you removed from this building so fast you won't know what happened."

Jac gave her a shocked look. "Wow, did you get up on the wrong side of the bed today or what?"

Sandy covered her face for a moment and took a few breaths. "You scare me to death every time, Jac." She dropped her hands into her lap. "I've been so afraid you would try something like this, as soon as you told me what you were doing." She shook her head. "I know you want to help but…"

"There was no other option, Sandy, they found another last night. We've hit walls in all directions…"

Sandy held up her hand, studying her for a moment. "Last night?" Sandy moved quickly to sit beside her. "You're lucky you didn't put yourself into a coma."

Jac kept her head down; trying to avoid eye contact with the men.

Brent leaned forward on the chair. "I know we're detectives and puzzles are kind of what we do, but if you two don't explain soon, my brain is going to implode."

Jac grinned at him and then covered her face. She sipped the tea again, an obvious stalling tactic. Hesitating, she glanced over at Reid. He sat opposite her, leaning forward on his knees, watching and waiting. "It's not that I don't want to explain, I just don't know *how* to explain." Slowly, she sat up and waited for her head to stop spinning. Exhaling loudly, she looked from one man to the other. "Every time I've tried to explain, it hasn't gone well."

Sandy sat there, watching her intently. Sandy knew what she could do, but from the look on her face, she didn't know how to explain it either. Turning her head, she looked at the men briefly and then back to Jac. "You could do what you did with me, I mean, once I stopped freaking out, I was okay."

Jac smirked at her. "Freaking out? I thought you were going to beat me to death with your black vase."

Sandy shrugged. "Reflex. What we don't understand scares us, so we tend to want to squash it."

Reid sighed. "Someone—anyone, explain *something*." He glanced at Brent briefly. "I am not a patient man." He held up his hand with his thumb and first finger an inch apart. "I have about this much left before I start growling."

By Jacqueline Paige

ANIMAL SENSES
1 *Heart*
2 *Scent*
3 *Passion*

MAGIC SEASONS ROMANCE
1 *Beltane Magic*
2 *Solstice Heat*
3 *Harvest Dreams*
4 *Autumn Dance*
5 *Winter Mist*

Dreams
Three steamy stories that started with a dream

Curses
Two tales of curses.

After the Silence
Volume 1 Bree

SINGLE TITLES
Solitary Witchling
Salvation
Café Serenity

Writing As: J. Risk

THE ALTEREALM SERIES
1 *The Huntress*
2 *The Seer*
3 *The Empath*
4 *The Witch*
5 *The Chronos*
6 *The Warrior*
7 *The Telepath*
8 *The Healer*
9 *The Kinetic*

Prologue

Jacinda didn't remember how she got home. Vague recollections of telling the cab driver her address, but the dizziness had been so bad, she could only focus on not throwing up inside the cab.

Once inside the front door, she slid to the floor hoping her parents weren't home. The pain fueled the dizzy feelings that made her feel as if she was floating. How could her skull be hurting this bad, but her brain feel like it was not attached?

"Jac?"

Her mother's voice was garbled. She tried to lift her head but couldn't find the strength. It happened again Mom, is what she wanted to say, but was afraid if she tried to talk, she would be sick.

"Oh no baby, not again."

She could feel her mother move her off the floor. She was sure she was moving her own feet, but couldn't be certain; she'd have to ask when she came to again. Just please don't let me throw up on my mother, she prayed silently.

"I knew going to such a large, public place was going to be bad. So many people, too many things to touch."

She recognized the worry in her mother's voice and could hear the fear. She'd had to try, just once more to know this would happen to her everywhere, every time. She had only wanted to help an old man get his stuff into his car. The vile thoughts in his mind were hidden behind a warm smile. How could she have ever guessed?

Jac felt her mom's gentle hands touch her forehead, trying to soothe the ache.

"I'll bring you a cool compress to help with the nausea. Just close your eyes and focus on staying calm."

Closing her eyes, Jac took a deep, slow, cleansing breath. Her head was still swimming. I'm such a freak. Wasn't it bad enough when they pulled me out of school? Thirteen and forced to live without a social life. She wondered if her friends really missed her, there hadn't been many phone calls in the last few months. I'll be the ghost no one ever sees.

Rolling slowly and carefully onto her side, not sure which was worse, headache, dizziness, or the urge to throw up all over the place. Her mother's voice carried from the hallway. She'd called her dad, which wasn't surprising. She supposed she was lucky her parents hadn't labeled her a mutant child and put her in some hospital to be studied. They were one of a kind, that much she knew. How many parents would be so accepting of a daughter that saw the past through furniture and other objects? Or that saw someone's emotions by touching them? Not many, she guessed.

"We'll get through this, Jac—no matter what it takes."

She relaxed and let the sleep she was fighting pull her under further. Her mother's words meant everything to her.

1

She stared up at the beams before her eyes rolled closed again, her arms were suddenly so heavy she didn't want to move.

Blinking she watched him as the tightness in her chest increased and her stomach heaved again—she couldn't struggle against it anymore…her face was so hot…so cold…

She focused on him through the blurriness for as long as she could and knew, somehow, they would find him…

Jacinda glared at the phone for a second and then put it back to her ear. "Thanks. Somewhere in the office really narrows it down for me, Sandy." She sighed. "I'll call you later. I am tearing this place apart until I find that stupid receipt." She snarled at the giggle on the other end of the phone.

"Don't get lost in there. You're supposed to meet me in two hours."

Jacinda stood up and studied the office, trying to decide on a starting point. "Yeah, yeah, I'll be there." Hanging up the phone, she put her hands on her hips and surveyed the piles of folders and papers scattered all over the two desks in the small, cluttered space.

Sighing, she grabbed a hair clip off the desk and twisted up her long dark hair. She frowned when it took two attempts to get most of it secured in the clip. One of these times she was going to give in and cut it all off. She rolled her eyes at her own thoughts. Of course, she'd been saying that for most of her adult life, so the chances of it actually happening were not high.

"Okay, so if I were a paid bill, where would I be hiding?" She hefted a box up from the floor. Being short did not help when your desktop reached your waist. Pulling out a handful of envelopes, she started shuffling through them. "Thanks for talking me out of a filing cabinet, Sandy—, boxes are so much more organized…" She smirked. Her friend probably meant for her to actually label the boxes and put them in the large closet. It was on her list of things to do. Eventually.

Halfway through the second box, she was mumbling obscenities for procrastinating with keeping some sort of order. Someday, an amazing client was going to walk through that door and money would fall from the sky. She smirked. Right, you ninny, the dust from the boxes has clogged your brain. Sighing, she pulled out more envelopes. Be careful what you wish for she thought as she dug in again.

By the time she reached the fourth box, she was ready to throw them all in a trash bin and light it on fire. "You'd think if I were one of the few paid bills, I'd be jumping right out of the box to be seen." She slid her hands lightly over the papers. Nothing. "Couldn't have a skill that would be useful when I needed it could I?" She sifted through another pile. "Oh no, I get the ability to see, but never anything I want…"

"Am I interrupting?"

Jacinda spun around towards the door. A tall, tailored blonde woman stood in the doorway. Her eyes were darting all over the messy room. Jacinda straightened up and brushed her hands off on her jeans. "No, of course not." She looked around the room. "Please ignore the mess. I've been—sorting things." The woman looked upset, but Jacinda resisted the urge to touch her and find out for herself if she truly was. "May I help you?" She watched her look down at a small card she held and then glanced around the room.

"I'm, uh, looking for a Jacque Brown."

Jacinda resisted the urge to stomp her foot at the masculine pronunciation of her name, yet again. Was the letter k really that necessary? "I'm Jac Brown." She studied her; there was something vaguely familiar about her. "Do I know you?" The blonde woman looked relieved.

"I'm Amanda Azaire." She held up the card and looked at the shorter woman. "I found your card in my sister's things." She glanced around. "Can—can I come in for a moment?"

Azaire. Why did she know that name? She motioned to the small table and two chairs in the corner. "Please, come in and sit." Azaire cosmetics. That was it. The woman's sister, what was her name? Lonie? Laura? Leslie …

"My sister Lanie is missing."

Lanie. She studied the woman sitting at the table looking suddenly lost and childlike. "Ah, right I helped your sister earlier this year." She sat down and chewed the inside of her lip for a moment. "What do you mean missing?" Large gray eyes looked back at her.

"I haven't been able to reach her for days." She wrung her hands together in her lap. "That's not like Lanie. She's never out of touch. We were supposed to be going away a few days, she would have let me know if—if…"

Not needing any sort of special abilities to know what came next, Jacinda reached over and set a box of Kleenex in front of her. She sat through the sniffling and tears for a few moments. "I don't do that sort of investigating Miss Azaire."

She sniffled again. "Please call me Mandy." She took a slow, shaky breath. "I know you don't, but I've already talked to the police." She took another breath. "And they say I need to file a formal report." She paused, biting her bottom lip for a moment. "To do that, I'd have to tell Daddy and if—if Lanie is just off somewhere, somewhere…"

"Oh, I see." Tell Daddy? She fought the urge to roll her eyes. Well, okay so Daddy running the largest cosmetics industry might run into some serious problems if word got out one of his children were missing, or worse, thought to be missing, when they're just off somewhere being human. "I really don't know what I can do."

She shrugged. "I was desperate and thought, I don't know— maybe you could check places and be a little less noticeable then if I were to do it."

Ah yes, being a nobody would of course be of assistance to someone like her… Jac's mind flew back to the bills that were due. Maybe being nobody sucked, but if she were paid for it, that would be a good thing. "I've never really done this sort of investigative research." She paused when a hopeful look appeared in the younger woman's eyes. "But I suppose I could poke around a bit and see if I can eliminate a few possibilities for you." The not so composed heiress lunged across the table and hugged her tightly.

"Oh, thank you. I don't care what it costs, I'll pay all expenses, just please, please find Lanie for me before Daddy finds out."

The younger woman's emotions flooded into Jacinda's mind, creating an instant tension. Trying to unwrap Amanda's arms, she smiled in a polite way. "Just let me get a pen and paper and I'll get some information from you, okay?" She stifled the urge to jump to the other side of the room out of reach, and shout, 'Don't touch me!' She managed to slowly walk over to her desk and dig out a notebook and pen from the clutter.

Forty-five minutes later, she looked down at the check sitting on top of the notes she'd taken. The photo of Elaine Azaire sat beside it. Now you do missing persons? The number on the check made her feel somewhat shell-shocked. Getting up, she walked over to the phone. Glancing back over to the check sitting a few feet away, she shook her head. The phone rang twice before her friend growled into the other end.

"You're going to stand me up, aren't you?"

Jacinda smirked. "With good reason." There was a chuckle on the other end.

"The only reason good enough would be a tall sexy man."

She grinned. "Or enough money to pay a few overdue bills. You think entirely too much about sex, lady." Sandy shrieked into the phone.

"You've robbed a bank?"

Jac snarled into the phone. "So funny, *ha ha.* No. I have a client and they paid me a lovely deposit."

"A deposit? What are you researching?"

She hesitated. "More of a who than a what."

"A person? You're investigating a person? Jac, you don't do people."

"Well, apparently I do now."

"Who?"

She chewed the inside of her lip. "I can't say."

"What? What do you mean you can't say?"

Jac brushed a pile of envelopes off her chair and sat down. "It's kind of complicated." She glanced at the advanced payment for what had to be the hundredth time. "And they're more or less missing."

"Oh. My. God. You took on a missing person case?"

"Well…" Why did she always stretch out those three words to emphasize her shock?

"I'll be there in ten minutes. Don't move."

She stared at the phone listening to the dial tone. She sighed. She was about to be reminded that people with any sort of ability that were different from the rest of the world were ridiculed and made fun of, or worse, studied like a lab rat.

Having been to a doctor once in her life regarding her special ability, she was examined like she was some sort of contaminated growth. They decided that her brain chemistry was out of balance. The solution, or so she'd been told, was a prescription to restore the balance and prevent the hallucinations. That appointment ended with her telling a rather alarmed doctor that he should tell his wife he was gay and save her the heartache to come.

Hallucinations my butt. She sneered. How could touching someone or an inanimate object bring about a hallucination that revealed emotions and events from the past?

Jacinda sighed and tried to push the feelings aside. It bothered her more than she cared to admit that she couldn't have a normal life, a normal job. She had tried many times and was not interested in putting herself through that again. She could count all the jobs she'd lost because of her gift. Being fired for not showing up or acting weird. Usually from seeing something she wasn't expecting, or the results of seeing something she didn't want. How many times had she regained consciousness with strangers standing over her, looking at her like she was a freak? Too many times.

She took a few deep breaths and brought herself under control. Glancing at the clock, she smirked. She should have timed it to see how quickly Sandy would get here. She loved Sandy, really. Sandy was her external conscience. She kept her from doing one stupid thing after another. She looked at the payment once more. What harm could discreetly looking around for someone cause?

She frowned, admitting to herself she was lying. The last time she had thought like that, things did not turn out well. She ended up having to move. Going through life being able to feel people's emotions and see things, that most times shouldn't be seen, was a hard life. That hard life had left her isolated and alone. She had also learned, the hard way, it was easier to be alone and live privately in a larger city than in a small town.

The last six years had been good, mostly since she met Sandra Gains, but her first thirty years had been trying. Learning to deal with emotions that weren't hers would cause her to be ill, or even pass out. Sandy had helped her find ways to cope, and as long as people didn't suddenly touch her when she wasn't expecting it, she was just fine.

2

Reid Merritt grit his teeth and tossed the file on his desk. He watched with an amused smirk as it slid across and off, landing in the trash basket. Leaning back in his creaky chair he flipped his scuffed boots up onto the edge of the desk. Close to a month now, he'd been digging through that folder, its content growing, but no solid leads found.

The six others that had been assigned to help him and his partner were starting to get on his nerves. There were only so many follow-ups and errands they could be sent on, before they were back here, standing in his office, looking at him.

Running his fingers through his shaggy brown hair he pursed his lips together. How many hours had he been sitting here cross-referencing? Sighing he crossed his arms and stared at the folder teetering half in the garbage.

The body found yesterday put the count at four. Four dead women, with not one thing in common except the fact that they were dead. The immaculately clean and neatly dressed bodies proved to be the only thing that told him it was the same killer.

He didn't even have an identity for number four. How could someone not have anyone missing them? He laughed quietly at himself. Do you have someone that would miss you? Nope. Not unless his annoying neighbor missed having someone to bore. It had been at least two years since he'd had anyone in his life that would notice if he was late home or never returned.

Shaking his head to clear the maudlin thoughts, he grit his teeth again. Drowning yourself in your own past wasn't going to help anything. Life happens. You pick up your sad ass and move on.

"Reid."

He looked across the room at the redheaded man leaning into the room. His friend and partner, Brent Jordan. "Yeah?"

Brent raised his eyebrows and looked at the folder. He smirked. "Captain Reely wants us in his office, *pronto*."

Letting out a breath, he kicked his feet back onto the floor. "On my way." He straightened his tall lanky frame and stretched. He was tired; the last month of chasing dead end leads was weighing him down. He should really take a few days off. To do what, he didn't know, all he had was work.

The only thing that appealed would be to spend a few days sleeping. When was the last time he'd really slept? He couldn't remember. If it wasn't his own mind waking him up, it was Brent phoning him with a crime scene address at every hour of the night.

Criminals should think about a union and sticking to office hours. Yeah. Definitely needed a day off thinking stupid shit like that.

He walked halfway across the room then turned and looked at the folder still sitting in the trash. "Should leave the damn thing there and let the janitor look at it, maybe he'd find a lead." Sighing, he strolled back over and picked up it. Without straightening the papers, he tossed it onto his desk and turned to head out into the hallway.

Reid walked into the office without knocking or greeting.

The balding man sitting at the desk smirked at him. "Good of you to join us."

Reid folded himself down into one of the chairs sitting across from the desk. "Anytime." He glanced over at his friend shaking his head. "So…"

The Captain sighed. "Do you have anything solid yet?"

Reid looked at his partner and shook his head. "No. We're just waiting on dental to see if we can give the fourth a name."

The Captain sat back and studied him. "It's definitely the same perp?"

Reid nodded.

He shook his head and looked at them. "I've never seen you have this much trouble finding a connection." He sat back and studied him. "The Mayor is hounding me. The press is getting harder to avoid, in case you didn't notice the reporters lurking at every door this morning.

"I noticed." Reid looked at Brent. He'd thank him later for no help. "Hopefully the identity of the fourth will open some doors."

The Captain nodded. "On that note, I have a few calls for you two, maybe it will open something."

Reid resisted the urge to moan. "Calls?" Where were the others that dealt with the dead-end calls?

The Captain sat back and studied him. The expression on his face reminded Reid of a parent assessing one of their children. "One call is from one of the families, a relative says they have something to tell us about victim number two." He handed a piece of paper to Brent, and then grinned at Reid. "The other is some type of investigator looking for a missing woman. From the brief description it could be your number four."

Reid's head popped up. "An investigator?" The Captain shrugged. "Aw hell. Give me that one. That's just what we need is some private investigator wanting to profit from this."

The Captain grinned and handed the paper over. "Your investigator has a photo of the missing woman."

Reid didn't even glance at the paper, just stuffed it into his pocket as he stood up. He nodded over to Brent as he headed towards the door. "Fill you in later."

Both men watched the door close. Brent smirked at the Captain. "Do you have any idea how tiring it is to keep up with those long legs?"

The Captain laughed. "Just keep thinking they're an asset when he needs to get to you fast."

Brent rubbed a hand through his short hair and grinned. "Very true." He pushed away from the wall he'd been leaning against. "We'll keep you posted, Cap."

~

Reid looked at the address. Jac Brown. He shook his head at

the error in the message. Mistakes like that could cost in his profession. He stopped at the stop light and waited, impatiently. He pictured this Brown character as a short round man, in glasses and last year's suit. He didn't have anything against private investigators; he had worked with a few that knew what was what, and more importantly knew when to let the cops handle things.

Although saying you are an investigative researcher was a new twist. He had to give the guy points for not following the norm. Checking the intersection briefly he accelerated when the light went green. Let's hope Mr. Brown was one of those that knew when to bow out and let the trained professionals deal with things.

Of course, he was way ahead of himself. He didn't even know yet if they were both dealing with the same woman. At this point though, he hoped they were. Then at least he'd know something he hadn't already known about this case this morning.

His phone rang. He answered it before it rang a second time. "Yeah."

"Most people say hello when accepting a call."

Reid grinned at his partner's voice. "Since when do I fit into that category?"

Brent laughed. "Okay, you got me there. Anyways, I was calling to see if you wanted to grab a beer after this never-ending day ends."

"We can."

Brent sighed. "Well, I just thought seeing as yesterday was your birthday and we were too busy working…"

"Oh yeah. Huh. Forgot all about it"

Brent chuckled. "You're the only person I know of that could forget their own birthday. Especially since you haven't even hit thirty yet."

"Biologically I haven't. In real time I'm in my fifties at least." He spotted the street he was looking for. "I'll call you when I'm done here, and we'll meet at Rusty's."

"Sounds good."

Reid pulled up in front of the building and turned off his car. He wasn't sure if he should be shocked or humored that he'd forgotten his own birthday. Twenty-nine. In some ways it seemed like he had been nineteen a few days ago, in others he was sure he'd never been young.

He sat and watched a group of boys messing around as they

went around the corner. Enjoy it boys, soon enough real life's going to begin and the fun is over. Well, maybe not all the fun, being all grown up had a few pleasant advantages. He watched them for a few more moments and wondered how they even walked with the way their pants fit. Times kept changing and he didn't want to understand most of them.

Picking up the note he stuffed it in his pocket and climbed out of the car. He walked into the building with long strides, the smile gone, emotions turned off, and headed straight for the stairs, not even giving the elevator a second's thought.

3

Jacinda stood back and admired her newly organized closet. That didn't take too long. Well, if you didn't count the four hours of sorting through the papers. Glancing down she looked at the last box. The only empty space left on the shelves had to be at the top. The top, she knew she couldn't reach. A step stool might have been a worthwhile investment. The two small chairs were too small. Glancing around she looked over at her desk chair. The other alternative was to drag a desk to the closet.

She stood on the spinning chair as it twisted back and forth with each movement. At least the wheels didn't turn very well, or she'd probably end up twirling across the room. Very slowly, she lifted the box up to chest height and waited to see if the chair was going to spin or tip. Slowly now, just another foot. She almost dropped the box when the chair turned quickly towards the left. Steadying herself she stood and looked at the shelf, it was now beside her instead of in front of her. She twisted her hip with a small jerk trying to make the chair turn back. When it did, she slowly reached out balancing the box.

A hand quickly went by her face and shoved the box up onto the shelf. She grabbed the shelf to stop herself from flipping off the chair onto the floor. Turning she looked into the face of the man with the greenest eyes she'd ever seen.

~

Reid smirked. "Your boss should buy you a stepstool." He stifled another smirk as he stared into large brown eyes that were looking at him, much like a deer caught in headlights. He grabbed the back of the chair to steady it and offered her a hand to get down.

She looked at his hand but reached past to grab his wrist where it was covered by his jacket. "Um, thank you." She pulled her hand away as soon as her feet were on the floor. She looked up at him, he had to be almost a foot taller than her.

Reid smiled. He found few women appealing, and she was one of the few. "I'm detective Merritt; I'm looking for Jack Brown." He looked around the tiny office noticing there were no other doors.

She pressed her lips together for a moment before offering him what could call a polite smile. "I'm Jac Brown. Jacinda, actually." She raised her eyebrows, almost daring him to comment.

"You're Jack?" She nodded at him and he could tell she was trying not to boldly grin at his surprise. "I guess I'm here to see you." He backed away a few steps and studied her for a moment in silence. This day was proving to be filled with surprises. "You called to inquire about a woman?"

She sighed. "They didn't have to send someone down here, simply answering my questions would have sufficed."

"Actually, I've come to ask you some questions." She stood there with her hands on her hips studying him. Why was it no matter the size or age of a woman, when they put their hands on their hips your first thought is uh-oh? His mind briefly hovered on the fact that the hips her hands rested on were nicely shaped ones, as far as hips went.

"Really?" She pulled the clip from her hair and dark long silky black hair fell almost to her waist. Grabbing the chair, she pulled it over to her desk. "What kind of questions?" She pushed the chair behind the desk and sat down before looking at him again.

He wanted to rush right to the point but having found out the hard way, he took his moment. Some people didn't deal well with the things he dealt with daily, so he took a few moments to think how to approach this. "Who were you looking for? Do you have a photo?"

She pursed her lips for a moment and studied him. "You

know I do."

She wasn't going to be easy to deal with. He tried not to smirk at her. "Yes, I do. Can I see the photo?"

She looked tense and gave him a very guarded look. "Why?"

Realizing this wasn't going to be one of those times he got complete cooperation, he walked over and sat in the chair in front of her desk. "Look, Miss Brown, I'm trying to do this as easy as possible." He smirked at her. "You're not helping."

~

Jac leaned on the desk and clasped her hands slowly in front of her. "I promised my client their name would not be brought into anything."

He frowned. "And why is that?"

She raised her eyebrows at him. "If I tell you why, then I'm basically bringing their name into it."

He blew out a long breath. "Well, I have a body in the morgue with no name. You show me the picture and I can see if we're talking about the same woman."

She sat back and looked at him. A body? Reaching over she opened her desk drawer and pulled out a file. She looked at him again; his expression was like he'd just told her he liked her shoes. His face was expressionless. Sighing, she opened it and handed the photo across to him.

He took it, glanced briefly back at her, and then looked at it again. From expression on his face, the body had an identity now. "It's the same person." He said quietly and then looked up at her. "Who is she? Why were you looking for her?"

She sat there silently for a few more moments. Elaine was dead? In all the hours she chastised herself for taking this client, she never once thought that this would be one of the possible outcomes. This was not how she wanted to tell Mandy she had found her sister. "I had done some research for her and her sister found my card and came to me," she glanced at the photo he still held. "She's been missing for five days now, and her sister is worried but didn't want to alarm the family."

"What's her name? What research did you do?" He pulled a notebook from his pocket as he spoke and opened it.

He was so emotionless in his questions. His tone was as if they were discussing the weather. "Azaire." He looked up at her quickly. She nodded. "Yes, Azaire industries. Elaine is the one in the picture." She clasped her hands in her lap for a moment. "Elaine's sister, Amanda came to me, because she didn't want to alarm their father or the media." He wrote something down then looked back up at her.

"And what research did you do for her before?"

She cleared her suddenly dry throat. "I researched the history and authenticity of a priceless armoire she was interested in purchasing."

He leaned back in the chair. Something in his eyes told her that she had just surprised a man that wasn't often caught unsuspecting. "You investigate furniture?"

"I investigate and research anything that anyone needs to be researched." She crossed her arms over her chest and glared at him.

"Why?"

Jac stood up and walked over to the small fridge in the corner. Reaching in slowly, she pulled out a bottle of water. Her hands weren't as steady as she'd like them to be. She opened it and took a small sip before turning back to answer him. "Because I have this ability to look at something and not see the same things everyone else does."

His eyebrows went up, but he didn't offer a comment, only continued to study her for several long moments. "You knew the victim?" She frowned but nodded. "Would you be willing to identify her, before I call the family?"

Jac's heart was racing. She definitely didn't want Mandy to be called down to the morgue. Was there a chance it wasn't Elaine? She'd never been involved in anything like this before. Could she walk into a space filled with death and not be overloaded with the emotions from the others that had been there before her? She honestly didn't know. She turned and studied him for a moment. "I'll get my purse."

He stood up and watched her walk back behind her desk. The look on his face wasn't one she could read, and for a brief second she thought of touching him to get a better sense of what he was thinking, but she decided not to.

Jac stopped when she reached the door and motioned for him to go ahead of her. "Do you mind giving me a ride? A friend dropped me off today."

He shook his head as he watched her lock the office. "Not a problem." He turned and headed down the hallway.

She felt numb as she glanced quickly up at him then back down at the floor. "Do you mind if we take the stairs? I prefer them."

"So do I." As they wound down the stairs, he pulled his phone from his pocket and dialed it. She kept walking. He spoke quietly into the phone. "Rusty's is on hold, I might have a positive ID."

She moved down the last flight, trying to stay ahead of him.

"On our way to find out." He must be talking to a co-worker.

He was now beside her again and looking down at her. "Meet us down there." He hung up the phone and stuffed it back in his pocket

When they reached a line of cars, he motioned to one. She climbed into the black car, careful to not touch anything then looked over at him as he put the key in the ignition. "I'd like to be there when, if you have to tell her family."

He shrugged. "Okay."

~

When they pulled up to the morgue entrance, she almost panicked. She took a few steadying breaths before she got out of the car. He stood by the entrance waiting for her.

Jac didn't look directly at him, just looked straight at the door as she walked through it. He led her over to a door then stopped before he opened it.

"Just give me a minute."

He went in and closed the door, leaving her standing there. Her first thought was she should have called Sandy to be here with her. Her second thought was, there was a better chance of Sandy passing out here than her. Sandy was one of those squeamish kinds of people that couldn't deal with blood or anything unpleasant.

"Hello."

She turned to see a large redheaded man standing a few feet away from her. "I'm waiting for Detective Merritt to come back out."

He leaned against the doorframe. "I'm his partner, Detective Jordan." He extended his hand. "Brent."

She quickly shook his hand, moving fast enough she wouldn't have a chance to pick up anything from him. "Jacinda Brown."

He offered her a friendly smile. "Why are you waiting for Reid exactly?"

"Oh, I'm here to see if the—I called the station looking for someone and they sent him to see me."

He grinned again. "You're the investigator?"

She nodded. "Is she— was she ..."

"Her appearance wasn't altered."

She swallowed. "Okay."

Reid opened the door and held it for her. "This way." She followed him inside.

She kept to the center of everything; being careful to not touch anything. In the center was a table with a white sheet covering what was obviously a body. She walked over and stopped two feet away. For one fleeting moment she wished she could lean on someone, just once to be able to use physical contact as comfort like other people. She sensed Detective Jordan step beside her and imagined his emotions were as frozen as his partner's, but still didn't chance resting a hand on him to steady her though this. Help me do this. She could do this.

A man, she hadn't even noticed walked over and stood on the other side of the table. He watched her for a moment and then reached and held the edge of the sheet. She looked at him, took a quick breath, and gave him a brief nod.

She watched as he slowly revealed blonde hair. When the sheet moved from the face, he stopped and stood there watching her. She looked at the lifeless face and remembered when Lanie Azaire had been so excited with the information she gave her. The face that was so expressive in every word as it was spoken was without life, without expression. It was her.

Jac was both sad and relieved. She licked her dry lips and turned away. "It's her." Without looking at anyone she quickly made her way back through the room. Pushing the door open with her forearm she hurried out.

"Elaine Azaire." Reid said quietly to Brent as he turned and went after her. When he finally caught up to her, she was back outside standing beside his car.

"I'm okay." She said quietly before he could get too close to her. "I just didn't want to stand in there."

He looked at her for a moment then nodded, walking around to the driver's side of the car.

4

Jacinda stood back as the two detectives spoke quietly to Amanda and Mr. Azaire. Amanda's father wasn't quite what Jac had expected, he didn't seem like he owned multi-million-dollar corporations. She chastised herself for the direction of her thoughts, she knew better than to stereotype people. He had handled the news better than Jac imagine she would have. He'd taken a few moments to console and comfort his remaining child and then had calmly asked for details.

Amanda turned and looked at her for a moment, before saying something to her father and walking towards her. Jac just prayed that the young woman wouldn't touch her. Grieving emotions were just as hard for her to block out as violent ones. She studied the teary eyes looking at her and clasped her hands in front of her. "I'm so sorry, Mandy, this wasn't what I wanted to..."

Amanda hugged her arms around her own ribs. She stopped a foot away from her. "I know." She wiped away a tear rolling down her cheek. "The detectives told us it wasn't brutal or," she took a shaky breath, "inhumane." She sniffled. "I don't know how they can say her being murdered isn't inhumane..."

Not knowing what to say to that Jac simply shook her head.

"You did find her though. Without you, we could have been left here wondering."

"She's right, Miss Brown."

They both turned to look at Amanda's father. He was still

steady and holding it together. Then again, you didn't build an empire not knowing when and when not to show emotion. He walked over and tucked his daughter under his arm.

"I'd like you to continue your investigations, Miss Brown." He glanced towards the other two men. "The detectives have just been telling me that Lanie's murder is not an isolated incident and they haven't been able to find anything to lead them to resolution." He paused for a moment and looked at Amanda. "Both of my daughters came to you and trusted you, so I do as well."

Jacinda glanced over at the two men and noted the surprised look on both of their faces. "I don't really…"

The composed tycoon placed a hand on her shoulder. "I insist."

She was swamped with the horrifying grief the man hid so well. Inside he was shaking and weeping for a child he obviously adored and was stunned she had been taken from him.

"Please," he said quietly as he dropped his hand from her.

She knew that was probably a word or tone this man rarely used. "I can see if I can be of help to the police, Mr. Azaire."

He nodded briefly. "I will pay for your time." He looked at the detectives for a moment before turning back to her. "I will also speak to the department head to clear this for you." He studied her for a moment longer and then turned back to the other men. "Now if you'll excuse us, we have arrangements to make."

She held Amanda's gaze for a moment and nodded to her. "I'll do what I can. Please call me if you need anything."

Mandy gave her a shaky smile before she turned to follow her father from the room.

Brent hissed out a breath. "I think we've been dismissed." Jac glanced at the other detective and knew by the expression on his face that she wasn't a welcome addition to their team.

Jac sat in Detective Merritt's car while they stood outside talking. Clearly neither were pleased she had been tossed into their domain. She felt numb. How was she going to maintain her own sanity while searching for a killer?

When detective Merritt climbed into the car, he glanced over at her. She turned and looked out the window. "I don't do people," she spoke quietly.

He gave her a blank look. "Well, you're in luck, I do."

~

Reid hovered over the Captain's desk as the man spoke into the phone. Glancing up he saw Brent was, as usual, not too concerned about the latest development. They couldn't possibly expect him to work with some random investigator on something as important as this case. If he was looking for stolen property, sure let her help, because it irked him to work on menial tasks like that. What qualifications did she have?

The Captain hung up the phone and let out a long breath he'd been holding before he looked up at him. "That was the Mayor, and before him was the top judge we have in our local judicial system." He stood up and leaned on the desk. "William Azaire rubs elbows with all the major influential people and my hands are tied."

Reid huffed out a breath. "Tied? So we're supposed to open our office and offer some investigator a warm welcome?" The Captain nodded. "What can she possibly find that we haven't been able to?" He turned to see Brent stand finally. "She doesn't even want to do this, so she'll probably fill her days looking like she's trying and getting in the way."

Brent put his hands in his pockets and shrugged. "It wouldn't hurt to have a new perspective on it…"

Reid's head jerked around to look at his partner. "A new perspective? On which part? That the victims are dead?"

Brent shrugged again.

The Captain stepped around the desk. "I don't particularly like it either, but because we've got nothing I can't barter with the Mayor and say we don't need help." He grimaced. "We don't have a choice."

~

Jacinda sat in the chair, making sure her hands didn't touch any part of it, and watched the two detectives in the glass office arguing with another man. If she were to guess, she would have to say the other man was their superior. She didn't need to guess why Merritt was clearly ranting to the other man. She knew she was the reason. Neither of them wanted an unofficial nobody to be included in a police investigation. She noted that Detective Merritt was objecting much more loudly than Detective Jordan. Although to stand back and observe the two officers, they were nothing alike.

Detective Jordan, while almost as large as his partner, had dark rusty, red hair and a pale freckled complexion. His personality was much brighter than his partner's. As if he heard her thoughts, he glanced out the office window and winked at her. She smirked.

Detective Merritt, on the other hand, had nothing close the sunny disposition of his partner. He was obviously a moody, internal, thinking type of man. She wondered if he'd always been that way or if what he was subjected to in his job had changed him over time. He had messy, brown hair that went just past his collar, and a tanned complexion, which only led her to believe he must do something in the outdoors when he wasn't slithering through a crime scene. She put her hand over her mouth to cover her grin. He wasn't a snake you silly woman, well, it was too early to tell if he was.

"Miss Brown."

She looked up to see the older man calling her from his office doorway. "Yes?"

He smiled. "Could you join us please?"

She quickly got up and walked into the office. The older man smiled at her as she walked in.

"Sorry to keep you sitting out there." He extended his hand. "I'm Captain Reely."

She hesitated a quick moment before taking his hand. Oh, he was a very compassionate man. "Jacinda Brown." She put her hands into her pockets and stood there. Detective Jordan was perched on the edge of his Captain's desk, looking like he had not a care in the world. Detective Merritt on the other hand stood leaning against the wall with his arms crossed over his chest, staring out the window.

The Captain sat down and smiled at her. "It seems you're going to be helping out, at the very insistent request of the Chief, who happens to be good friends with Mr. Azaire." He clasped his hands on the desk. "I don't have to tell you how rare this is, and I'm sure I don't need to tell you to not overstep any boundaries."

Jac nodded and smiled at him. "I truly don't know if I'll be of any help at all, but I can assure you I won't get in the way." She ignored the hiss that came from the man leaning against the wall and focused on the man in charge. "I can do most of the research from my own office…"

Detective Merritt snapped his head up and looked at her. "Our files don't leave here."

She looked calmly at him for a moment. "Then I guess I'll have to stay here." She smiled sweetly at the Captain. "Is there a computer I can use?"

The Captain nodded. "Just ask if you need anything and my men…" He glared at the scowling man for a second, "*will* be happy to help."

She nodded. "Okay."

The Captain looked at Detective Jordan, who was smirking. "Take her downstairs and show her what you guys have."

He nodded and stepped over to the door, motioning for her to come with him.

She smiled at the Captain. "Thank you." Detective Merritt hadn't even moved from his brooding stance. She pursed her lips and walked over to him. Standing with her hands on her hips she waited until his green eyes focused on her. "Just to set the record straight, detective, I don't want to be here anymore than you want me to be here." With that she turned and walked through the door. She tried not to giggle at the big grin on Detective Jordan's face as she passed him.

5

She listened carefully as Detective Jordan led her to the doorway of a large room filled with desks and busy people. He skimmed over the names of people in the room and explained what they were doing, not that she'd remember. She was shocked to see that so many people were working on the case, if she'd heard right there were six other officers and three people basically just answering tips calls. What are you doing here, Jac? She stood on the other side of the door hoping he wasn't going to tell her to go in and jump right into things. She couldn't work surrounded by this many people. Her mind was so preoccupied, causing her to miss whatever he said as he started walking away and going down the stairs. She caught up to him in time to hear that she would be working in the basement with him and his partner.

Reid took his time following them downstairs. He stopped to talk to Daniel, who was waiting for calls on the hotline. There hadn't been any calls that led anyone to believe anything would turn up. He looked over the latest list of dead-ends that had been checked out. Having nothing else to stall from going downstairs, he sighed and walked out the door.

By the time he got downstairs, his partner was setting files on the large table, and she was typing into her cell phone. He glanced at Brent who shrugged and sat down by the table.

Jacinda's phone rang before she could send the text message. She knew it was Sandy before she even answered it. Her friend was into her rant before she got a word spoke. "Sandy, I don't care if it's a dinner for the Queen of England, I can't make it tonight." She sighed and nodded. "Yes." She sighed again. "I'll call you if I get done earlier." She nodded. "Fine." With that she hung up the phone and stuffed it back in her pocket. She clasped her hands behind her back and looked at Detective Jordan. "Sorry."

He shrugged. "No worries." He motioned to the files on the table. "That's all we have at this point."

She nodded and sat down at the table. "Okay."

~

Brent got up from his desk; after an hour of silence. Other than a few questions from Miss Brown, no one made a sound.

Reid hadn't moved from his desk either. Brent walked over to look at the monitor his partner was studying. His eyebrows shot up when he saw what his partner was doing.

The normal database searches were open, and his brooding friend was digging into Miss Jacinda Brown's past. Before he could be considered an accessory, he walked around and leaned against the desk. Reid looked up at him and shrugged. He cleared his throat. "I'm going to go get a coffee. Anyone want anything?" Reid nodded and looked back at the monitor.

"No thanks." Jac looked at him for a second then back down at the papers she had spread out on the table.

When she heard him leave the room, she glanced up to see what Detective Merritt was doing. Satisfied he wasn't paying any attention to her, she picked up the photos she'd been flipping face down as she read.

Victim one, as it was labeled, she now knew as Clair White, age thirty-six, brown eyes, red hair, five foot ten inches and one hundred fifty pounds. Number two was Theresa Woodward, age twenty-seven, blue eyes, brown hair, five foot six inches and one hundred sixty pounds. The third, Desi Sloan, age thirty-one, brown eyes, black hair, five foot nine inches and one hundred forty-five pounds. She had only skimmed some of the reports and print-outs in the file, not understanding what the toxicology and laboratory tests actually said.

She didn't need to read Elaine's file to know these women had nothing in common. They lived in different areas, were of different social statuses, their jobs weren't similar, just as their appearance wasn't.

All had been dressed differently, and although it sent a chill up her spine, she knew from the reports that their clothing had been immaculately clean, if not freshly pressed.

She looked over at the detective. "There is nothing remotely the same about these women."

He looked up from his computer. "Yeah, we know that." He sat back and clasped his hands behind his head. "Now would be the time to impress me with that ability of seeing things no one else does."

Her shoulders dropped as he threw her words back at her. "Really? I wasn't aware that I needed to impress you." She stood up and stretched.

He smirked. "If you can find anything remotely close to a lead, I'll be impressed all to hell."

"Mmhmm." She blocked him out and walked around the room. "You'd have checked places of employment, clubs, memberships…" She paused to look at him as he nodded. She sighed. Right now, she was wishing she hadn't accepted that check from Mandy Azaire. "Have you…" Could it be as simple as money? "Checked financial activity?"

He dropped his hands down. "It's all in those folders; we checked credit card transactions, payroll…"

"No." She walked over and stood in front of his desk. "Not the usual things. Financial as in, inheritances, windfalls, trust funds…" She frowned. "Or if they've been in the news in any way, well, except Miss Azaire, I'm sure she has."

"Can we keep her?"

They both looked around to see Detective Jordan walking back in carrying two coffee mugs and a bottle of water. He handed one mug to his frowning partner. "She's thought of a few avenues we haven't ventured down."

He turned around and handed her the water. Even though she had said she didn't want anything, she opened it and took a drink. "So, give me a computer and I'll do the one thing I do very well, research."

Detective Merritt still hadn't said a word; he just sat there watching her. He watched Brent lead her over to a computer in the corner.

Jac sat down, careful to not let her hands rest on the desk or chair. This was something she knew she could help with. She watched the detective type in a password then motioned to the keyboard.

"Database programs we access are in the menu."

"Thank you, detective Jordan." She rummaged around in her purse. If she put on gloves to type, she'd probably be escorted out. She'd have to type fast and not let her hands linger on the keyboard.

He smiled. "Brent." She beamed up at him as she pulled her hair with quick motions up into a hair clip.

"Thank you, Brent."

Reid looked over at her for a minute as she began entering names into the search.

Brent sat back at his desk and grinned over at him. "I'll call the Captain."

Reid just nodded without looking away from her. She may have found the lead. She turned and looked over at him.

"How far back in the news am I going?"

He shrugged. "Start with six months."

She nodded and turned back towards the screen.

~

Jacinda wanted to bounce as she waited for the news articles to print. She grabbed them as they came out one by one.

She spun around to see Detective Merritt watching her from his perch on the desk. She glanced at the board the two men had flipped over, it had all the women's information on it. She'd seen things like this in movies and always thought they were kind of neat, but to see one in front of her wasn't a good feeling. She looked over it slowly; four women were now listed like pieces of a puzzle. She stared at the pictures of them and wondered how necessary it was to have a photo of each dead woman pinned up here. She would never forget their faces.

Detective Jordan spoke softly beside her. "It saves time going through files." She just nodded but continued to look at the board. "What did you find?"

She turned and looked over at the other detective. and then down at the pages in her hand, almost having forgotten them. "Oh." She held out the first page to him. "Desi Sloan liked to gamble, she won big four months ago."

He glanced at it and handed it over to Brent, who was now standing beside him.

She held out the second page. "Clair White's wealthy aunt passed away, also four months ago." This time he took a bit longer to read it over before passing it to Brent. Glancing at the next page she frowned then handed it to him. "Theresa Woodward's much older husband passed away six months ago and left her a huge estate."

Detective Merritt nodded and handed the page to his partner. "Elaine Azaire had a trust fund?"

Jac nodded and handed him the last page she held. "So, now what?" She was very pleased with herself and couldn't help wanting to rush to the next step.

Brent was holding the phone already. "We get bank records."

Detective Merritt stood there looking down at her. "I'm impressed." He said it quietly. She beamed a 'told ya so' smile at him. "We stopped after employment and credit searches, none of them seemed to be worth much."

Jac looked at him for a moment. Was he pleased she'd found something he hadn't thought of or did he just say it because he thought that was what she wanted to hear? She lowered her head and tried not to smirk and doubting he'd ever say something just because someone wanted to hear it. Clasping her hands in front of her she glanced back up at him. "It was a long shot."

He picked up the pages she'd handed him and held them out to her. "Put your leads on the board."

She gave him a startled look as she took the pages back. Deciding there wasn't a proper comment to make, she said nothing.

As she was writing under Elaine's news clipping, the Captain came through the door. "I didn't intend the two of you to hold her prisoner down here." He glanced at Detective Merritt. "Do any of you realize the time?"

Jac looked up at the clock. Sandy was going to be fuming, not only had she missed the reception, but the dinner as well. The Captain came and stood by her. He tapped the newspaper article. "Your doing?" She nodded. "Good work, Miss Brown."

She tried not to show how pleased his praise made her feel. "Jac."

He smiled at her. "Jac." Turning towards Detective Merritt his smile faded. "Break for the night and let Jac go home and get some rest."

The somber detective just jerked his head once acknowledging he'd heard.

Jac walked back over to get her purse and let the three men discuss the findings, her phone buzzed in her pocket. Probably Sandy unleashing the hounds of hell she thought as she answered the phone with a smirk.

"Miss Brown?"

"Yes." The caller sniffled.

"It's Mandy Azaire."

Jac stopped in the middle of the room. "Mandy? Is everything all right?" Clearly, not the most intelligent thing to ask her with the circumstances. All three men turned to look at her. Another sniffle.

"Yeah, I'm just—I wanted to tell you I just feel better knowing you're going to help."

Jac put her head down and stared at the floor. "I'm going to try." There was a long pause.

"I guess it's too soon to ask if you know anything."

Jac looked over at the men watching her and sighed. "Actually, I'm going to need some financial records of Lanie's, if you could…"

"Hold on, Daddy just walked in."

She listened to the muffled conversation on the other end and almost dropped the phone when the male voice came out of the earpiece.

"Miss Brown. It's William. What do you need?"

She sent a pleading look to the three men. "I, we, believe the possible link may have something to do with your daughter's trust fund Mr. Azaire."

There was a long pause. "I was afraid of that."

He sounded defeated. She glanced at detective Merritt, who

was writing quickly on a file folder. He held up the folder, with a number scribbled on it. "Would you be able to fax any records or statements to the detectives?"

The man on the other end cleared his throat. "Yes, first thing in the morning. Let me get a pen."

"I'm really sorry to …"

"Don't be. Give me the number." His voice was all business again.

Brent held up a piece of paper with the fax number on it. She gave it to him and was ready to hang up when a quiet little girl voice came back on.

"Thank you, for everything."

"Try to get some rest, Mandy."

"I will, Jac."

She hung up the phone and stood there looking at the three men. Turning quickly, she busied herself with straightening up the notes she'd had beside the computer. She didn't want them to know how hard this really was for her. She was helping find a killer, and she truthfully didn't want to have anything to do with it. Sighing she picked up her purse. She couldn't walk away now either, she had to help.

6

The morning was filled with people coming in and out of the basement office. She smirked each time Detective Merritt had gotten up to close the door; he really wasn't a people person.

Usually, random surfing, about anything would help her think, come up with something. But it wasn't working today, and she was so tired of the flashing ads on every page she opened. If she saw one more dating ad, she was going to—

She snapped her eyes back to the screen. Still looking at it, she pushed her chair back and slid halfway to the center table. Jumping out of the chair she quickly opened one of the women's folders.

She scanned down the credit card statement with her finger. Holding the finger on the one statement, she flipped through the pages in the next file. Quickly going down the pages bouncing back and forth, she felt her heart pick up, she might have something, the first six numbers were different, but the last five were the same.

An arm came around behind her and flipped open the next file, turning quickly to the credit card statement. Standing there with a finger on one printout, she scanned down the list, doing the same comparison. "It's the same."

Brent came over and looked at the pages under her hands.

Jac was almost bouncing. "If the last file…" She stopped as Brent flipped it open and tossed the credit card statement in front of her. She looked up at the men for a moment, and then grabbed a pen and began circling the entry on each of the four statements. She set the pen down and looked up at Detective Merritt. "How do we find out what those charges are for?" She chewed her lip. "The amounts aren't the same but the last of the numbers are."

She paced over to the computer. "I think the first parts are membership numbers."

Brent was already holding the phone.

Detective Merritt followed her over and looked at her monitor over the top of her head. "Membership to what?"

Jac turned and looked up at him. "I think, maybe internet dating." He gave her a questioning look. She shrugged. "They were all single…"

Brent smirked at his partner. "Some people want to be in a relationship." He turned towards the table, ignoring the scowl from his partner, and grabbed the first credit card statement.

Reid put his hands in his pockets. If he had looked for a year, he probably wouldn't have come up with that. He knew at some point he was going to have to admit that having her help was a good thing, but he still wasn't ready to say it out loud. Shrugging he grinned down at her. "I don't care where this leads, if they're even closely connected, I'm buying dinner."

Brent put his hand over the mouthpiece of the phone and laughed. "Now he's impressed."

~

Reid read over it again. He was expecting, well he had no idea what, but not this. Jacinda's name only came up once in any database he searched. Apparently, she'd discovered a smuggling ring, with antiques. He shook his head. What was with this woman and furniture?

He read the last part once more. Jacinda Brown-Straton assisted in the location and apprehension of— The names were irrelevant. The part that kept snagging his attention was her last name. Why did she only use Brown when her last name was clearly hyphenated? Had she been married? Nothing came up in the registrar. Why would she relocate on the other side of the country? Abusive boyfriend? How did he find out?

"Your turn to go get coffee."

Reid looked up at Brent's smirk. He glanced at the clock and sighed. "I guess it is." He stood up and glanced over at the woman half slumped on the desk clicking through one site after the other. He walked over and looked down at her. She looked bored. "How many hits?"

She sighed and looked up at him. "Over four hundred million."

"Ouch." He smirked. "Why don't you give it up until we have a name at least?" He turned. "Want anything from the lunchroom?"

She sat back and sighed again. "Tea, black, please."

He nodded and walked out.

Jac paced around the office as they waited for the call from whomever Brent had phoned for the information. She was so nervous. What if these turned out to be completely different and didn't link anything together? She walked over and looked out the tiny basement window, then glanced over at Brent who sat calmly at his desk waiting for the coffee. "Why are the two of you hidden in the basement?"

He grinned. "I like to think it's because we're important we get a big space to ourselves, but I think it's to keep us out of the Captain's space."

She smirked. "Are cases like this the only ones you two do?"

He shook his head. "We really don't work for any one area of the department." He grinned, showing her his teeth. "We get the cases that no one else can figure out."

She was impressed. Obviously, they were both very good at this. "Oh." Turning she wandered back over to the window for the umpteenth time.

Reid walked back into the office and stopped as soon as he'd seen the expression on Jacinda's face. She was standing behind his desk. He hadn't closed the file on his desktop.

Brent walked over to him wincing and quickly took the one mug from him. "I'll, uh—be back."

He watched him almost run from the room. Coward, he thought with a smirk.

"I'm researching, trying to find a lead—for you, and you're

researching my past?"

Okay, so it sounded bad when she put it like that. "I like to know who I'm working with." He set the cups down on the table, safely away from the angry woman. She was definitely angry, no guarding that emotion from showing.

She stepped around his desk. "Then ask!" She hissed at him.

She stood there glaring at him with her hands on her hips, almost daring him to push her further. And the part he had trouble swallowing was she looked so appealing, he wanted to go over and hug her. His own thoughts jolted him into action. He walked with long strides over behind his desk. Appealing? Where had that insane thought come from? She looked like she was going to rip his head off and hand it to him. "Why did you move away?"

She flung a hand towards this computer monitor. "Can't you read? I'd helped convict the son of a very powerful man and didn't want to spend the rest of my life looking over my shoulder."

He frowned at the article on his screen and then looked over at her. Asking was making her angrier. "Is that why you changed your last name?"

She put her hands back on her hips and dropped her head down to look at the floor. "Partially, Brown is a very common name and looks much neater on a business card than Brown-Straton."

Every word she spoke came out in a clipped controlled voice. He was sinking here. "Why do you avoid people?" Her head popped up and brown eyes burned into him.

"I do what?"

"Avoid people; you walk through a room making sure you're close to no one."

Her eyebrows shot up. "Do you like being close to strangers, Detective?"

He jammed both hands into his pockets and shook his head.

"Are we finished?" When he nodded, she spun and grabbed her purse heading towards the door. Brent was just stepping through it. "I'm going to get some air." She snapped as she moved past him.

Brent rolled his head towards his stupefied looking partner. "That went well."

Reid blew out a breath. "Yeah."

Brent looked back out the door she'd stormed through.

"Maybe, you should go try to fix it?"

Reid shrugged.

Brent grinned and walked over to stand in front of him. "Okay, setting aside that whole pride thing, which you seem to have gotten more than anyone's share of, she has gotten us further with this case in two days than we've gotten in a month." Reid just stood there and looked at him. "*And* the Captain will hit the ceiling if she walks out when the Chief, Mayor and all those other big guys find out she quit because you're an ass."

Reid grinned to that. "Well, they all know that, so that shouldn't be too shocking." He let out a deep breath. "I'll go talk to her." He unclipped his gun and set it on the desk.

Brent smirked. "Is that so you don't shoot her or so she doesn't beat you with it?" Reid gave him an annoyed look and walked out. "Bit of both," he mumbled to himself.

Jac stood there leaning against the wall with her hands tucked in her pockets. That's wonderful, having a little tantrum. Stupid man. The part that would bother her the most would be that she'd lied again. Okay, there was truth in her answers, but she was so tired of having to lie to hide what she could do.

She remembered the strange looks people gave her when they realized. They ranged from complete disbelief to looking at her like she was some sort of mutated monster. She almost preferred those that thought she was insane and needed to be medicated.

She sighed and pulled her phone from her pocket. Times like this called for one thing. She quickly sent a message to her favorite head doctor and waited for a reply. She grinned as the message came immediately. 'session with an unorthodox method of alcoholic beverages, tonight, my place'

Where would she be without Sandy?

Reid strolled to the side of the building; hoping she was still close by. An apology would be harder if he had to chase her down. Apology? That was something he didn't do often. Why had he been in such an off mood lately? Was it the endless dead ends in the case? No, cases didn't affect him like this. He stopped walking suddenly. It started from the moment he walked into her office to see her surfing on a chair. He smirked, watching her twist and wiggle her curvy little body hadn't been too difficult to take.

Things turned rocky the moment she had opened her mouth to speak. Since when did a female affect him like this? Shaking his head, he walked to the corner of the building.

She was leaning against the back corner smiling at her phone. He hoped this was a good sign he wouldn't get kicked when he invaded her moment. It was hard to tell with most women though, so he approached her with caution.

Stuffing the phone in her pocket she watched him walk towards her with a cautious look on her face.

When he got close enough, she straightened. "Don't apologize please." He slowed his pace and studied her. "I know you'd somehow turn it around to blaming your profession and make me appear like an overreacting twit, so an apology you don't mean is just going to upset the balance more."

He stopped and looked down at her. "Technically, it does lead back to my profession, not to mention how rare, if not strange it is, to have someone without a list of degrees a mile long tacked onto their name working so closely with us."

She smirked. "I'm almost positive you'd check out the degree holders' backgrounds too." He offered her a shrug. "I'm really trying not to invade your space detective." She took her phone back out of her pocket and looked at it before putting it back. "This is just as far out of my comfort zone as it is yours."

He frowned. That was it right there. His comfort zone. He actually felt uncomfortable and awkward in her presence. He ran a hand over his scruffy face, and then looked down at her somberly. "I am sorry I dredged up your past." He let out a long breath. "I get why you're upset by it." He held up a hand when she started to speak. "But in self-defense, people in my profession end up dead if they're not suspicious of others."

She bit her lip giving him a thoughtful moment. "I'm sorry I flipped out." She looked in his eyes. "I've had to do a lot of explaining and defending my every step and you happened to hit a real sore spot."

He pulled the phone from his pocket when it buzzed but didn't answer it. "I really didn't intend to stir anything up." He watched a breeze blow the dark hair she'd freed across her face. He completely forgot what he was planning to say next as he watched her pull the long hair to one side and look back up at him. He grinned. "So, are we good now?"

She smiled. "You're still buying dinner."

He laughed.

"Don't either of you answer your phones?"

Both turned to look at an exasperated Brent.

He waved a piece of paper at them. "We've got the name." He stopped and looked at Jac then grinned at his partner. "And dinner is on you."

Jac grabbed the page from his hand. "I was right?" She looked at them. "I was right. Internet dating site, Love Quest Dating." She smirked.

Reid dropped a hand down on her shoulder. "Keep this up and the Captain is going to be giving you a badge."

She stepped back and grinned. "Or your job." With that, she quickly headed back toward the front of the building.

Brent pursed his lips together and turned to him. "Ha!" He started walking in the direction she'd gone. "She just keeps getting better all the time."

Despite the smile on his face, Reid growled at the other man. "Shut up. We have work to do."

When the two men entered the office, the look of surprise crossed both of their faces when they saw the Captain standing talking to her. Their superior turned and smiled at them. "It seems to be heading somewhere now." He gave Detective Merritt a brief look. "And just in the nick of time too, I've run out of things to tell the Mayor and stall the reporters."

Brent walked over to the fax machine and held up a few pages. "Financial info is starting to arrive."

Jacinda almost held her breath. "Whose and what does it say?"

Brent handed a few pages to his partner and then looked up at the Captain. "Jac's theories are right on the money, literally." He scanned the second page and then looked over at her. "Grab the marker." She jolted but did it and stood in front of the map board waiting. "Theresa Woodward transferred six thousand dollars a day before she died." She wrote minus six thousand under victim two's information. He looked at the next page and sighed. "Eight thousand transferred by Desi Sloan the day of her death." He held the pages out to the Captain and turned towards Reid.

Detective Merritt looked up from the pages and then over to where Jac was standing. "Miss Azaire transferred nine thousand the day of." He watched her falter for a moment, but then she turned and wrote it down. He glanced at the fax machine. "We're still waiting for the last statements to arrive."

Walking over Detective Merritt took the marker from her as she stood there looking at the board. He wrote 'LQ' above each of the amounts she had put on the board. He turned and looked at her when he was finished.

She realized then that they were all looking at her. "Sorry, it's just, well my first thought is these women are dead for a few thousand dollars."

He didn't seem surprised by this, as she was sure he'd witnessed even more pitiful excuses for crimes. "And with your work, we'll find out who and put a stop to it." His voice was softer.

She took a deep breath and then nodded. "Right." Without looking at the others she walked over to the computer and sat down. "Let's see what Love Quest dating is all about." She typed in the web address and hit enter. She almost rolled her eyes when the page opened to pink hearts and scrolling testimonies of cuddling couples. Oh please, was her only thought.

The detective looked over her monitor. "You've got to be kidding."

The Captain and Brent walked over to look. Brent grinned at him. "Just the kind of place you'll be most comfortable investigating."

Jac looked up at them and rolled her eyes. "Just give me a little time and I'll be able to explain the system." She jumped up and went over to the table and grabbed the credit card receipts. She turned around and then stopped when she realized the three men were watching her.

The Captain cleared his throat. "I'll get out of your way." He walked towards the door. "Make sure I get regular updates."

Brent nodded. Turning toward his partner he grinned. "Guess we'd better start trying to find out where that money went."

Brent's large partner just nodded and walked back over to pick up the faxed statements. "I'm going to try to find a registered owner for that site first." Brent was already at his desk typing data into his computer.

He glanced over at the woman who was flying through pages on the web. "Am I buying takeout, working through kind of dinner?" He knew both Brent and he would stay in the office and not want to leave now that they had some leads.

She paused and looked at him. "Pizza works for me."

Brent chuckled. "Better all the time."

7

The empty pizza boxes sat on the edge of the table. Jac got up and located where she'd left her water and stretched a few times. She looked over to see Brent frowning at his computer. His partner didn't look any happier where he sat glaring at his keyboard. "I've gone through as many male profiles as I can stand to look at today." Really though, had she expected just looking at a few faces, she'd spot one that called out 'killer'? She stretched again hoping this would signal to them she was tired and more than ready to leave.

Brent looked up first. "Figure out the site?"

She shrugged. "Well, I had to buy a membership to it, to get all the way in." She rolled her eyes. "Of course, my profile is not filled out and is completely unpublished and as soon as this is wrapped up, I'll be closing *that*." She took another sip.

Brent grinned at her. "Not interested in a *love quest*?"

She almost spit her water out. She sputtered a few times then gave him an exasperated look. "No."

He chuckled. "You and my partner have a lot in common on that ground then."

His partner's head popped up. "Ignore him." He gave her an exaggerated look. "He believes everyone has a soulmate out there somewhere."

She gave him a serious look. "Oh, so do I." Then bit her lip. "Of course, in my situation, my soulmate is in some faraway place, and his ship crashed on the way to find me, now he has amnesia and can't even remember why he was on the ship in the first place."

Detective Merritt laughed. "Okay, everyone is getting a little tired." He stood up and stretched. "Show us what you've found out and we'll cue you in on anything we don't know yet."

She quirked an eyebrow at him then shrugged. "It's nothing too fabulous over here either." She walked back over to the desk and put one knee on the chair and clicked the mouse. "Basically, you sign up, full address and all that, you get a membership number." She clicked on her account. "The highlighted areas other members can see, the gray boxes are only for me and the company." She pointed to one highlighted box. "I had to create a username." She sighed. "Then to communicate with other members I send a message through their message box, if anyone replies it's in the inbox."

Detective Merritt stood behind her reading over the screen. "So they can see what city you live in, age, height and whatnot and your username and that's it?"

She nodded. "Pretty much, any other information I'd have to personally tell them."

Brent was beside her now. "Like financial information." She nodded again then turned to look at the fax machine as it began printing.

The detective sighed and went over to get the printout. "Last financial statement." He pulled it out and studied it. "It doesn't tell us much we haven't figured out trying to trace the account."

Jac watched him walk over and write four thousand under Clair White's name. "It's increasing." She stated quietly. He turned and gave her a blank look. "The amount, each time it's increased."

Brent stuffed his hands in his pockets. "Yeah."

She shook her head to snap out of the sadness she felt coming. Turning back towards detective Merritt she held up her hands. "Did you manage to find out anything?"

He nodded slowly. "I have the office address for the website, but no names yet." He ran a hand through his hair. "I'll take a run over there tomorrow and see if I can't get something." He looked at Brent. "Did you get any further than you were an hour ago tracing the money?"

Brent leaned against the desk and crossed his arms. "Not

much, most places are closed now, so I can't go any further tonight." He shrugged. "The same account was used, but now it's been closed, all funds wired elsewhere." He looked at the board for a second. "I couldn't get anything more than a post office box because the account has been closed." He glanced back at him. "I'll give that bank to the Captain and see if he can pry something further from there. Which will take court orders and all that because of the banks privacy policy." He sighed. "So really I have twenty-seven thousand dollars transferred from an account and wired to a place I'm having trouble getting to."

Brent's partner frowned. "Chances are when you do find it, a fake ID and another post office box will come into play." Brent nodded and then stopped and looked at the door.

Jac turned around. "Sandy?"

She walked slowly into the room, her short blond curls bouncing with each step. "I thought I'd come and pick you up." She walked towards the redheaded man and extended her hand. "I'm Dr. Gains, a friend of Jac's."

He smiled and shook her hand. "Detective Brent Jordan."

She looked over at the other man leaning who nodded to her from where he stayed leaning. "Detective Reid Merritt."

Sandy smiled at them then turned to Jac. "You didn't tell me they were so good-looking, hun."

Jac chuckled and shook her head. "So you thought you'd come to pick me up, huh?"

Sandy shrugged. "And check things out."

Jac looked at the two men. "Forgive my friend; she's sometimes too nosy for her own good." She watched Brent spin the map board around to the blank side and wink at her. "If we're done beating our heads against the keyboard for tonight, I'd like to go home."

Detective Merritt pushed away from the wall and nodded. "Absolutely. I'll pick you up in the morning and we'll start again."

She nodded and chewed the inside of her lip. "I'd like to think tomorrow is the last day, but maybe I'm dreaming a little."

Brent shrugged as he bent down to turn off his computer. "Never hurts to dream."

Sandy beamed a smile at them. "Pleasure to meet you both." Then followed Jac from the office.

Brent turned and smiled at Reid. "Well, the doctor was a bit of—nice."

Reid laughed. "You shouldn't drool on their feet it looks too eager." Then he frowned. "A doctor of what I wonder."

Brent stopped and glared at him. "Don't even think about it. I thought Jac was going to throw the monitor at you when she saw her life on your screen."

Reid looked shocked then smirked. "Yeah, I was a little worried for a minute too." He flicked off the light switch. "Meet you at Rusty's?"

Brent sighed longingly. "Exactly what I hoped to hear you say."

~

Jac flopped back into the large white cushions on Sandy's couch. "I don't know if I can do this."

Sandy was sprawled in her graceful way across the chair. "You are doing it."

"I know, but so far I've been able to stay out of everyone's reach." She took another sip of the weirdly flavored cooler. It didn't taste like any kind of breeze to her.

"You could get lucky and stay hidden in the dismal basement and not have to do anything other than the computer work."

Jac moaned. "Wrong. That's not going to happen; we're going to Elaine Azaire's funeral tomorrow afternoon." She held the cold bottle against her forehead to distract herself from the panic.

Sandy raised her eyebrows at her. "How did that happen?"

"Mr. Azaire would really like the three of us, *investigators*, there to check people out and keep an eye on things." She rolled her eyes at her friend. "The only things I'll detect are feelings of grief, just before I pass out on the floor from the overload."

Sandy sat forward on the edge of the chair. "Does he think the killer is going to show up at the funeral?"

"I don't think so, I hope not." She slumped back further into the cushion. "How am I going to make it through a funeral, Sandy? People hugging, consoling, touching—" She glared at her own hands then back to her. "Grief is one of the hardest emotions for me to deal with. It sucks me in to the point where I can't break free from it. It's worse than hatred and vulgar emotions. I don't want to pass out in front of a church full of people."

Sandy set her glass down and sat on the floor in front of her. "Keep your hands out of reach, most definitely, you've gotten really good at that. Most people probably won't look twice at you. Stay close to the detectives and most will avoid you all together."

Jac let out a slow breath trying to calm herself. "I'll try. I don't know how I'm going to completely avoid it though." She glanced at the clock. "I really have to get going."

Sandy stood up slowly. "You haven't really mentioned the two detectives." Her voice was filled with suggestion.

Jac set her drink down and picked up her purse. "Please, don't start match-making again."

Sandy paused with the keys in her hand and sighed. "I'm not trying."

"You know a relationship just slows me down. I'm a better person on my own."

Sandy looked at her for a moment. "You only say that because you've had a few bad ones."

Jac laughed. "Bad ones? They were actually great, or so I thought." She shrugged in a nonchalant manner. "Of course, being able to see when a man cheats on you turns it bad fairly quickly."

Sandy leaned against the counter and looked at her for a moment. "Would that be better if you didn't have the ability to see? I've counseled a lot of women that are constantly wondering if their partner is faithful. It consumes them to where their health is affected. Examining every moment and trying to find a sign that their fears are reality."

Jac rubbed her hands over her face and groaned. "No, it's not better, not really, then I'd be in a relationship with a cheater and not know it." She shrugged then lied to her only friend. "I'm happy alone." Her friend shot her an exasperated glare. "Seriously." She shrugged. "I've never been in a relationship where I could actually be completely myself, Sandy." Jac studied the floor for a moment. "For years, I wished for a nice man who I could share a life with." She looked into sad knowing eyes. "One that would accept all of me." She shrugged again. "I gave up on that fantasy and accepted my reality *long* ago. I'm happiest alone."

Sandy smiled at her. "I can tell this conversation is going to go as far as it usually does." She grabbed her purse from the counter. "Come on I'll take you home."

Jac laughed. "You make it sound like I'm difficult." Her friend just rolled her eyes and opened the door.

~

He knew Brent was watching him as he sat there silently swirling the beer in his glass. "You know you could pretend to not be thinking about work."

Reid grinned. "I could but we both know I would be."

Brent sighed. "Tell me you're at least brooding a little bit about Miss Jacinda Brown."

Reid took another drink and debated on getting another drink. "Why would I be brooding about her?"

Brent leaned across the table. "At least thinking about her?"

Reid shrugged and set the empty glass down. "I am, she's taken this case further in a few days than we managed in three weeks."

Brent laughed and shook his head. "Yeah, she has. But that's not what I meant. I couldn't help notice the two of you spark off each other. She's hard not to stare at all the time, don't you think? Hair up, hair down, doesn't matter she's just vibrant..."

Reid's eyebrows shot up. "Spark? There are no sparks, it's more like stubborn meets determination. And if she's so *vibrant*, why are you trying to put her in my lap then?" His mind, whether he wanted it to or not, automatically pictured her cuddled into his lap. Great, imagery he didn't need.

Brent set the glass down and leaned back folding his arms over his chest. "How long has it been since you did something other than work?"

"A few years I guess." He saw the look on his friend's face. "Oh no, let's not discuss that dead end. I am not falling into that trap again." He fought to keep the memory of finding his fiancée with another man from filling his head, of course it did anyways. Until that one moment, he'd thought love completed a person and bettered them. He was wrong.

Brent gave him an exasperated look. "Not all women are like your ex."

Reid pulled his phone from his pocket and looked at the time. "That's fine, but I'll save the happily-ever-after for you and the rest of the male population. I think I filled my quota in that area." He stood up and grinned. "I'm outta here, we have a long day tomorrow."

Brent raised his glass in a toast then drank the rest. "Yeah. I love funerals, a group of strangers crying together, should be fun." He frowned and got up.

8

She put a change of clothes in the back of the detective's car. She climbed in and shrugged. "If I'm going to go to an heiress's funeral, I'm not wearing my jeans."

He grinned and looked down at the black suit pants he was wearing.

She took a moment and noted he'd shaven and his hair was less shaggy looking. "At least we're on the same wavelength."

He pulled the car out into traffic. "I'm going to drop you off then go over to the address we have for the dating office and see if I can dig anything up."

"Don't you need a search warrant for that?"

He smirked. "Sometimes, unless people feel an uncontrollable urge to cooperate."

She chewed her lip. "Can I come with you?" She shrugged. "Maybe I can help find that urge."

He glanced at her for a moment, then back to the road. Grinning, he nodded. "I don't see why not."

Jac was relieved to see it was an office like any other. She'd been afraid it would be all hearts, or something as equally tacky. Standing out of the way as she watched Detective Merritt speak quietly to the receptionist. Clearly, the mousy older woman wasn't intimidated at all with his badge or willingness to help him in any sort of way.

She moved closer to hear the exchange.

The round-faced woman gave him a skeptical look. "Don't you need a warrant to pry into files? It's against our privacy policies to simply hand them out to anyone."

The detective straightened to his full height, an annoyed look on his face. He put his hands in his pockets. "I could go and get a warrant, but this is a very time-sensitive situation."

"What situation?" The receptionist demanded.

Jac bit her lip to stop from grinning. She could see the muscle in his jaw twitching, no need to touch the man to see how annoyed and frustrated he was becoming. She stepped in front of the desk. "Perhaps I could be of assistance, Detective Merritt?" She offered a polite smile to the woman sitting there.

He studied her for a few seconds then shrugged, motioning for her to go ahead.

Jac smiled at the woman again. "It is your job to do data updates and list maintenance?" She nodded abruptly. "Okay Ms…"

"Mrs. Oster."

Jac smiled. "Mrs. Oster, I wonder, you see—" She turned to look at the detective and grimaced. Walking around the desk she leaned over and spoke quietly to the other woman.

Reid stood back and watched. He wasn't sure what she was whispering to the woman, but he could see the look of shock come into her eyes as her mouth dropped open, then snapped shut to be replaced with an angry scowl.

"The bastard."

He heard her hiss.

"What are the women's names again dear?"

Almost shocked, he pulled out his notebook and flipped to the appropriate page before handing it to Miss Brown, a solemn look hiding her twinkling eyes.

Reid wanted to smack his hand down on the counter and demand why now, as she was typing quickly, she was cooperating? But when the printer started spitting out multiple pages, he decided his pride would just have to suffer without an answer.

Jac took the pages from Mrs. Oster. "We'll let you know as soon as we know."

Mrs. Oster nodded quickly. "Please, then I can remove his account." She smiled in an unfriendly sort of way. "And possibly smack him for being such an inconsiderate bastard."

Jac nodded and smiled again. "Thank you so much, and rest assured, we didn't get this from you."

Reid just nodded to the older lady and followed Jacinda out.

He waited until they were in his car again then smirked at her. "Going to share how you did that? Because I know you didn't tell her we suspected a murderer.

Jac looked at him for a moment then grinned. "STI." She said softly then smiled at his puzzled look. "I simply told her that we suspected one of their male clients had a sexually transmitted disease, and the common links were the women we were representing." She chewed her lip. "We are representing those women and I'm sure in the client database, somewhere, someone has an STI." She shrugged at him.

He thought for a moment before he started the car. Grinning at her finally he whispered. "Remind me to stay on your team."

She laughed and patted the printouts in her lap. Looking over at him she frowned. "So, now the bank account is closed, do you think that's the end?"

He'd asked himself the same question half the night. "I don't know."

Reid reached over and grasped her hand, giving it a light squeeze. "We're going to find him." He stated softly.

She could only nod in response. Her whole being was swamped with emotions. She could have looked deeper but decided selfishly she just wanted to absorb the strength of his surface emotions, and use that to help her blunder her way through this investigation.

She looked down at their clasped hands, noticing how small her hand looked in his. Heat flashed through her system, but before she could react, he'd released her hand and gripped the steering wheel. "Thanks." She said almost in a whisper. "When this is finished, I am never straying away from furniture again."

He smirked at her words then shrugged. "That's too bad, you're better at digging stuff up than half the people trained for it."

Jac was shocked, she couldn't help it. He was not the type of man to just toss out compliments, he'd use them sparingly and only when absolutely necessary. "Thank you." She could feel her cheeks heat and was embarrassed that he would see she wasn't comfortable with kind words.

He glanced at her a few more times during the drive but didn't say anything more.

~

Reid wasn't surprised to see reporters lurking by the station. They could only be stalled for so long. "Shit." He mumbled.

Jac turned and glanced at the crowd, then back to him. "How do we get in?"

He studied the frightened look in her eyes for a moment. "I'll go jump into the chaos you go around back." She just nodded before opening the door. He didn't wait until she'd pulled her clothes from the back, just took long strides into the melee. A reporter he preferred to stay clear of came sauntering out of the thick of the crowd. Nicole Anderson. A man-eater would be the polite term for her. She was a six-foot, blonde, black widow spider, as far as he was concerned. Giving her a 'not today' look, he breezed past her like she wasn't even there.

~

An hour later the three stood in the basement office staring at the three new, male names written on the board.

Brent sighed. "I was really hoping for one name."

"That would have made it too simple," His partner said quietly.

"Simple would have been good," Jac said, irked. Walking over to the computer she sat down. "Let's take a look at their profiles."

Both men moved to stand behind her.

She logged into her profile and typed the first name in. "I give you Wrangler dash zero one, aka Will Denton." She patted the list of printouts from love quest. When his profile loaded on the screen she sat back and looked at it. "He looks like a snob."

One of them chuckled from behind her.

Brent reached over and moved the mouse to print the page. "I'll take the snob then."

They all stared at the screen as she brought up the next profile. "Meet Ladies Servant or Mister Paul Saint-John."

"How old does it say he is?" Detective Merritt moved closer to the screen.

Jac scrolled down the page. "Thirty-nine."

He lifted an eyebrow. "Leaning close to forty-nine I'd guess." He studied the picture a moment more. "Print it, I'll check out Mister-older-than-I'm-saying."

Jac nodded and click on print. Looking over at the printout she sighed. "That leaves Sincere Man or Robert Wise for me." Both men stood behind her as the profile opened on the screen. She grimaced. "He looks like an axe murderer."

Brent chuckled. "Well, if the killings were brutal, I think he'd be our guy."

Jac turned and looked up at them. "So, where do I start looking?"

Brent looked at Reid for a moment, they both turned back to look at her. He tilted his head to the side and smirked at her. "Where do you think we should start? Seems to me that what things we don't think about, you try first."

She knew her mouth dropped open for a second before she bit her lip in concentration. "Well. I would start by seeing if they were available on the dates of the killings?" Brent nodded. "I mean before digging really deep, let's see if we can eliminate at least one of them."

Detective Merritt frowned at her. "You are after my job, aren't you?"

She laughed. "No, definitely not. You can keep it."

All options she checked that would take Robert Wise out of the country came back empty. He hadn't taken a plane, train, bus or ship anywhere. Not good for him so far, she thought. Brent's chair scraped the floor as he stood up, making her jump. Great, she was going to have a heart attack and die before she got through this. She watched him walk to the board and cross off Will Denton's name, and then he wrote France #2 #3 beside it. She didn't need to ask what that meant. She knew that eliminated him for the times Theresa and Desi were killed which meant they were down to two possible suspects.

Turning back to the computer, she sighed and stared at the search applications. Heart attack. She frowned, then opened the health search program and typed in the name. Waiting impatiently, she sat and stared at the screen. A hospital came up on the screen.

Her shoulders dropped. She wasn't sure if it was realizing he wasn't a suspect or worry that unless the third name on the list came up with something, they were back where they started.

Pushing her chair back, she got up and walked over to the board. Picking up the marker, she crossed off Robert Wise, writing hospital #3 beside it. Turning she saw Brent sigh and rub a hand over his face in frustration. She turned to look at Detective Merritt still searching the final suspect, his focus still on the screen in front of him. When his hand smacked the desk, she jumped and glared.

He grimaced. "Sorry." He walked over to the board and looked at it. "Mr. Saint-John was not anywhere else on any of these dates, and he's a bad, bad boy." He met Jacinda's curious look. "He's married and living with his wife and two children." Her jaw dropped. "*And* registered with a dating site."

Brent puffed out his cheeks or a moment, and then exhaled. "None of that makes him a killer, sadly." He glanced at the clock. "We're going to have to postpone the chat with Mister Cheater, we have a funeral to go to." Jac's shoulder slumped. "I know, I'm not looking forward to it either. It's bound to be a media circus." He grabbed his jacket and headed to the door. "I'll go see the Captain to tell him what we have so far."

Jac waited until he left then turned to Detective Merritt as he was pulling his jacket off the hook. "Um, I don't want to be in front of the media." She clasped her hands and looked down at them. "I don't need the people I left behind to find me."

He studied her for a long silent moment, "We'll keep you out of the limelight."

She smiled. "Thank you." She took her change of clothes off the coat hook she'd placed them on. "Just give me ten minutes."

9

Jacinda stood at the back of the chapel, careful to stand behind Brent. It wasn't as crowded with reporters as they'd feared, but there were enough cameras to make her want to stay out of sight. At least they weren't allowed inside.

She had been stunned by the number of celebrities and other influential people attending. Actors, judges, government officials, and so many corporate giants she felt even more invisible and unimportant than she did on a normal day. Just what was she doing here, she wondered?

So far, she'd been able to avoid being touched, yet dreaded the moment Mandy noticed her. She knew that not making direct eye contact usually worked to keep her unnoticed. What she didn't know was how she'd not look at Mandy or her father.

Reid walked back to join them. Brent was scanning the room looking for anything out of the ordinary. Jacinda looked completely withdrawn. He liked to think it was just being out of her working clothes, and she was as uncomfortable as he was in a tie but knew the change in her demeanor happened once they'd arrived at the funeral.

When she'd walked out to the car at the station, he'd been stunned by the change. Of course, Brent had whistled, making her smile. She'd pulled some of her long hair off her face in a complicated weave, leaving the rest hanging down, surrounding her shoulders like a cloak. A basic black skirt suit hugged her nicely curved body, then and he discovered that she'd been hiding very nice-looking legs under her jeans. She'd even taken the time to put on makeup, which made her huge brown eyes appeal to him even more.

He looked over Brent's shoulder down at her. "If you're trying to hide, it's not working. I could see your shoes on the way over." She looked up at him, those huge brown eyes made his heart jump. Frowning, he reached over and played with the long hair falling off her shoulder. "You really don't like being surrounded by strangers, do you?" She shook her head, not taking her eyes off his hand touching her hair. "Sorry." He dropped his hand. "You don't have to come."

Jac's eyes shifted to the Azaire's, surrounded by people she'd only ever seen in the newspapers. "I'm pretty sure my invitation was more of a summons." She whispered, ensuring that no one would overhear.

Reid put his hands in his pockets and glanced briefly over at the millionaire sitting at the head of the casket. Holding his elbow out to her he smiled. "Let's do this, so we can sit at the back and blend in."

She looked up at him and blinked. "Because being the tiny man you are, I'm sure you blend in easily." He shrugged and held his elbow out again.

She took a deep breath and put her hand through his elbow. She felt basic male protectiveness, and that she could bear in this situation. "Thank you, Detective."

He paused and looked down at her. "Reid."

She gave him a brief smile and then glanced over to see Brent walking closely on her other side. "I feel like a rock star surrounded by bodyguards."

Brent grinned down at her. "You're our star." He nodded politely to some in the crowd as they walked past, and continued to speak quietly. "We may not have wanted your involvement, but we'll lock up anyone that tries to take you from us."

She looked up at Brent, then, up to the man whose arm she clung to. "Um, thanks?"

Reid looked down. "Are you ready?" Her hand tightened around his arm. "Just hang on and no one will grab at you." She just nodded. Brent gave him a skeptical look over the top of her head. Reid just set his jaw and gave a quick nod.

Jac was surprised to see William Azaire stand up when they reached him. He nodded at the people surrounding him, and they politely walked away. He looked down at her.

"Thank you for coming, Miss Brown." He nodded to the men. "Detectives." He looked around the room for a few moments. Turning to his daughter he reached down and held her hand for a second. "I'll be back in a moment, sweetheart." She just nodded.

Brent followed behind the millionaire, but Jac pulled Reid closer to the grieving sibling.

Mandy gave Jac a somber look. "Thanks for coming."

Jacinda's heart felt like it was too big for her chest. "How are you doing, Mandy?" The blonde woman looked down at her hands holding the tissue.

"We're going to be okay."

She said it in a way that made Jac think she was trying to convince herself.

Mandy looked at the detective and then back to her. "Daddy said we'll go away after this to regroup."

Jac nodded. "That sounds like a good idea."

Mandy nodded and sniffled. "I know Daddy is waiting to talk to you, so I won't keep you."

They turned to walk away.

"Jac?"

They stopped and Jac turned to look at her.

"Are you closer?"

Jac just nodded, not knowing exactly what to say.

Mandy wiped her eyes with the tissue then nodded at her, barely holding back the tears. "Good."

Taking a shaky breath, she clung to the detective's arm and walked with him over to Mr. Azaire, she decided to remain quiet as she didn't know what to say.

Reid leaned down to whisper, "If you could leave that arm attached, I'd really appreciate it." Her heart was beating out of control, a combination of nerves and dread running through her system,

"Sorry." She loosened her grip. Chewing her lip, she glanced quickly at Mr. Azaire then back up to the man trying to lighten the mood. "I'd rather be at the dentist."

He winced. "Are you a sadist? The dentist?" He blew out a breath. "You're doing fine; we're almost out of here."

She looked briefly at Brent as they stepped in front of the man that hadn't stopped examining her as they approached. She wished it was how much leg she was showing, but knew the tycoon was looking to her for resolution and justice.

When William stepped closer Jac fought the urge to bolt. She felt the detective hold her hand tighter against his side in silent support.

"Miss Brown. I've been trying not to phone and harass you and the detectives every hour." He put his hands in his pockets and studied her. "Did the information I sent help?"

She knew he was struggling with every word. "Yes, it did."

"So…"

"We're a lot further ahead than we were." Reid straightened to his full height and looked at the other man, demanding focus. Azaire looked at him for a long moment before nodding. Reid cleared his throat. "Miss Brown has been working long hours with us and has brought us closer than we would have been on our own." Jacinda looked up at him. She knew Brent felt the same way, but she was surprised to hear him say it.

William Azaire stood, silently processing this information. Jac could see the emotions going through his eyes. He looked back to her suddenly, the pleading clear to read.

"Do you need anything—anything at all, to…"

She reached with her free hand and placed it on his arm. "No, we're fine, sir."

He nodded and patted her hand a few times. "We're going to be going away for a while; I'll call you with the number."

She pulled her hand back and clasped it with the hand still looped through the detective's elbow. "We'll let you know as soon as we know."

He glanced past her shoulder then straightened, a cooler and in control expression coming over his face. "I have to get back to Amanda." He nodded to the three and quickly walked away.

Jac blew out a long breath then glanced at Brent. "Are we done yet?"

Brent grinned. "Soon." He motioned to Reid. "Let's go sit in the back and watch who comes and goes."

Reid nodded and turned with her still attached to his arm to walk to the back of the room. He looked down at her as she navigated, carefully not touching anything or anyone but him. "Did you want a cup of tea?"

She released his arm and sat in the chair as far in the corner as she could. Blowing out a breath and nodded. "Yes please, tea would be nice." He left to go get her one.

Brent sat down beside her. "I take it you'd be happier if I didn't leave you here alone until he's back."

She smiled. "You would be correct."

He leaned a few inches closer to her. "Do you have a people phobia?"

Jac suddenly wanted to tell him everything. "It's very hard to explain, I'm just much more comfortable away from groups of people."

He nodded thoughtfully. "You have a lot in common with Reid." They both turned to watch him work his way back to them. "Inside he's growling and gnashing his teeth at every one of them."

She put her hand over her mouth and laughed quietly. "Whereas on the inside I'm running the other way and screaming don't touch me."

He chuckled and patted her knee lightly. "We'll get you out of here in one piece." He stood when Reid was standing beside him with a cup in each hand. He was almost glaring at the cups. Brent winked at her. "Whereas I, on the other hand, feel the more the merrier." He wandered off towards the most crowded area of the room.

Jac wrinkled up her nose at his partner. "Sadist."

Reid watched his partner walk away, chuckling. He sat down and handed her the cup. "Did I miss something?"

She took a sip and grinned. "We were discussing how I would like to run out of here screaming don't touch me and that he likes lots of people."

Reid snarled. "Yeah, he's always trying to drag me into crowded places."

She tipped her head to the side and looked at him. "I figured with your size crowds wouldn't be a problem, can't you just look over everyone's head?" She looked at him with her tongue in her cheek, hiding a smile.

He dropped his head down and grinned. "In most cases. I just don't like being surrounded by people I don't know."

Jac sighed. "Yeah." She surveyed the room, trying to relax a little bit.

Reid checked his watch. "When Brent gets back, we'll get him to hold our seats in this hidden corner and go find a quiet spot for a few minutes." She gave him a surprised look. "We still have over half an hour before the service begins." She just bowed her head in response.

~

Reid opened the third door and looked inside. This one was truly empty. He glanced around for witnesses, then motioned for her to go inside.

Jac stepped in and took a few breaths. "I didn't realize the cameras would still be outside."

He frowned. "Oh, they're not going to miss a chance to get a picture that might be newsworthy or at least gossip-worthy."

She leaned back against the closed door, looking around the tiny room. "Well, it's not as fancy as the last two, but at least it is empty."

He cast a quick glance at the chairs shoved against the wall. "I think this is some sort of closet."

She looked around again. "I think you're right, but I don't care." Running a shaky hand over her face, she rolled her shoulders.

Reid noted the strained look on her face. She was honestly that uncomfortable? He went to stop in front of her. Leaning one hand beside her on the doorframe, he looked down. "Do you want to go?"

Jac rested her head back against the door, looking up at him thoughtfully. "No, that would be admitting I'm a coward."

He gave her a serious look. "Who cares what anyone thinks?"

Jacinda chewed her lip and regarded him again. "I meant to myself."

He smiled down at her. Pride was something he understood. He didn't know why he was going to do this, hadn't thought of it prior to this moment. And he knew he'd question it many times after. But—

Reaching slowly with his other hand, he put a finger under her chin and slowly tipped her face up to look at him. Her eyes watched his, waiting for him to say something. He intended to say something, but his mind seemed to have paused.

Slowly, giving her more than enough time to stop him, he lowered his head and brushed his mouth lightly over hers. There was something inviting in the way her mouth responded that gave him no choice but to kiss her again, lingering for a few seconds longer.

It wasn't a movie scene kiss, just a brief connection. But there was something about the way she leaned there against the door, not touching him but accepting and returning his kiss that caused his heart rate to pick up so quickly he thought she would hear it. He lifted his head and looked down at her. Brushing his thumb lightly over her cheek he straightened slowly. She just stood there with her head tilted up toward him, eyes wide open.

Jac finally blinked, and then let out a breath as if she'd been holding it. The look in her eyes made him want to kiss her again.

Reid leaned a little further away from her and smirked. "I did not intend to do that, I was going to…"

Both turned their heads when the music started playing. He glanced quickly at his watch. "We have to go now unless we want everyone to watch us walk in."

"Uh, no." She jerked away from the door and pulled it open.

Reid grabbed her hand and pulled her through the door behind him. Each time they passed someone he slowed.

Reaching the outer doors to the chapel, he stopped and put his hand in his pocket. Offering her his elbow, they walked through the doors and calmly walked over to Brent, and took their seats.

Brent gave Reid a look filled with questions. Then he looked at Jac, she was smirking with her head down.

"I thought you two had bailed on me," he whispered quietly enough not to be heard.

Jac smiled at him and then shrugged. "No. Your partner dragged me into a closet to kiss me." She looked to the front of the room quickly, a smirk on her face.

Reid's eyes widened. Brent knew his mouth was hanging open, but he couldn't stop it.

Reid dropped his head down, hoping he would appear to be grieving.

Grinning, he put his hand over his mouth for a moment then

glanced at the woman sitting there looking somberly towards the minister at the front of the room. "Troublemaker," he said quietly. The corner of her mouth twitching was the only indication she had heard him.

Lifting his head, he chanced a glance at Brent disbelief still on his face. Reid shrugged quickly then turned his attention to the front of the room.

~

They didn't go to the burial. As soon as the services were over, the three found a side door and slipped out without bringing any attention.

The ride back was silent; Jac sat in the back watching out the window. She knew that Brent was looking over at his partner with a question not spoken every few minutes.

She leaned forward. "Thanks for all the help back there. I wasn't sure I was going to get through it." She glanced to see green eyes watching her in the rearview mirror.

Brent turned and gave her a mischievous grin. "Apparently, one of us was more helpful than the other."

Smirking she decided to put him out of his misery. "Okay, I might have fibbed a bit. I was not dragged into a closet." She looked at the green eyes watching her, then back to Brent, now leaning so far back he was almost in the back seat. "I needed a few minutes not surrounded by people, so we found a storage room and stood in there until the services started."

Brent continued to examine her silently. Turning he cuffed Reid on the shoulder. "You jackass." He laughed. "You were happy to leave me thinking you were ravishing poor Jac in the closet."

Reid leered at him then grinned. His green eyes then glanced in the mirror again and met hers. He checked the road again before bouncing briefly back to her. "I didn't start the rumor." She smiled then returned her gaze out the window.

Brent looked around at her again. "So, are we putting in a few more hours at the office, or calling it a day?"

Reid regarded her in the mirror. "You up for a bit more investigating?"

Jac nodded and glanced briefly at those serious eyes. "It's

more eliminating isn't it?"

He nodded abruptly. "As long as it takes us closer each time, I don't care what we call it."

She nodded, "I could do a few more hours today."

Brent rubbed his jaw. "I want to go speak with our only suspect."

Reid clenched his jaw and then glanced back at her with those green eyes again. "You okay with hanging back at the office and digging up some more possibilities?"

"That's fine. I have no idea where else to dig right now though."

Brent turned towards her. "I have pages and pages of information on the possible location of the wire transfer. Detective McGowan has been working on it but hasn't gotten far. It's numbers and some branch information, you could work on discovering where it went."

She shrugged. "I'll try."

10

An hour later both men walked back into the office. Reid stopped and smacked Brent on the chest, frowning at him.

Brent grinned and walked to where Jac was sitting. "Tell me you've cracked the case."

She stood up slowly and bit her lip. "No. You?" She watched as Reid walked over to the board and cross off the last name. She sighed when he wrote confirmed alibi and the numbers one, two and three at the top. Puffing out her cheeks, she waited. "Well, I know where the money went." She knew it wasn't a fantastic announcement, but it was better than none.

The two men stood there watching as she started walking slowly around the office with her hands on her hips, looking at the floor. She looked up when another detective walked in holding papers. Reid met the other man halfway and took them from him. Without a word he placed them on the table.

Brent went over to the table and picked up the sheet she had written the branch address on. He snarled and handed it to Reid. Neither man was happy to find out it was at least two hours away.

Jac paced for another minute before stopping to study their expressions. "There is another option." She bit her lip. "It's going to be very time consuming." She picked up the printouts from the dating site. "Going over the profiles on these lists." She sighed. "Just because the names don't match, doesn't mean the pictures on the profile won't."

Reid tilted his head and looked at her. "What, like one could have more than one profile?"

She waved her hands around. "Something like that." She cast a quick look at the papers in her hand. "This list includes all contact through the site, so it's only logical to assume the women would message them a few times at least, before agreeing to meet them." Pacing to the table, she set the papers down. "If we look at Clair's list, there are," she quickly counted the number in the list. "Thirty-five contacts, some of them are the same person two or more times, some of them she met, some she didn't." She looked up to see both men looking at her. They weren't getting it. "If we start with the names on the list that she wrote more than once, then met up with at least once, then compare the profiles pictures, it might be the same man." Both men were obviously skeptical. "The only other option is for me to spice up my profile and publish it."

Reid shook his head. "You are not going be bait."

Brent leaned on the table and studied the list. "Not a good option at all."

Brushing her hair back, she shrugged. "I would at least be doing something until you can get the videotapes from the wire location." Brent gave her a curious look.

"Videotapes?"

She pointed to the pages on the table. "The company the wire was made through boasts that they have surveillance equipment, at every location to ensure client safety."

Brent regarded Reid then turned back to her. "Next time mention videotapes first."

Jac frowned. "Oh sorry, I thought I had.

Brent grinned. "I'll get on this right now." He turned and jogged out of the office.

She closed her eyes and rubbed the back of her neck.

"Run this profile pictures thing by me one more time."

Stopping, she opened her eyes. "It wouldn't be too hard to have more than one profile, I mean the usernames are laughable, chances are they'd use their own photo and just wear glasses or a hat or something to change up their look if they had more than one profile." He shook his head. "What?"

Reid smirked. "I don't think I would have come up with that in a million years."

She sighed. "I just thought…"

"It's a good idea, let's start looking." He picked the first victim's sheet and rolled a chair over to the computer she used.

Jac sat down and opened her computer at the login. She typed in her username and was entering her password when he chuckled beside her.

"Mystic Lady?"

She eyed him. "It was the first original thing I could think of."

He nodded. "It's good, creative." He looked at the screen then back at her again. "Is that your real age?"

Jac leered at him. "Yes, why?"

He grinned. "You don't look it."

She sat there and looked at him for a moment, trying to decide if he was being sincere. "Thank you." Turning, she picked up the page and scanned down it to find the username that came up more than once. Typing it in she waited for the profile to open. She sighed and looked at him. "If I publish my profile…"

"No." He didn't turn to look at her, just picked up the sheet and checked off the profile she had brought up. He turned back towards the computer screen. "Can you leave that picture open and look at another one?"

She nodded and glanced at the list for the next name. She typed it in. No? That was it? No discussion, just no. She chewed her lip and waited for him to check off the name before typing in the next one.

Brent came back in and leaned on the back of her chair. "Tape is being sent to us in the morning."

She turned to look up at him. "Let's hope there's something on it."

Brent shrugged. "We'll know tomorrow." He stretched. "So, what are we doing here?"

Jac turned back to the computer. "Not discussing why I can't put my profile out there and see what happens."

Reid studied her and then stood up. He looked at Brent, being less then helpful by raising his hands in surrender. Turning her chair, he leaned down, so he was face to face with her. "We are not discussing you using yourself as bait. We don't operate that way here. This is not a movie or a soap opera." He continued to look at her face. The kiss came to his mind and he mentally cursed himself for even thinking of repeating the move.

Jac scowled at him. "Obviously, or I would turn it off and read a book instead." She studied his eyes, looking for a break in his expression. She broke the eye contact and lifted her hands in exasperation. "Fine." When he straightened up, she turned and looked at Brent. "My brain has hit overload can we just call it a day?"

Brent glanced over at the clock and slumped his shoulders. "I'm more than willing." He to him. "Reid? Call it a day?"

Reid regarded the time then nodded. "Maybe we'll get lucky tomorrow and get a picture of who we're looking for from the tape." He watched Jacinda for a silent moment. "I'll give you a lift home."

She picked up her purse and shook her head. "No need, I'm heading over to my office, to see if I still have one."

Reid frowned. Was he looking for an excuse to be alone with her? "Are you sure?" She just nodded and headed into the bathroom to get her bag of clothes. "Do you want a lift in the morning?"

She stopped and smiled at him. "Please. Same time?"

He smiled back and nodded.

She waved over to Brent. "See you tomorrow. Have a good night." She walked quickly out the door.

Brent turned to him. "Does that strike you as odd at all?"

Reid gave him a puzzled look. "What?"

Brent laughed. "What?" He studied him. "Who are you and where have you put my partner?" He shook his head. "She's determined to publish her profile; you pretty much lay down the law and she just smiles and waves?"

Reid cast him a blank look. Stopping he glanced back to the door she'd gone through, then back at his partner. "Shit." He had to get his brain back on track.

Brent pointed at him. "Now you're back."

Reid grabbed his jacket off the chair he'd tossed it on. "She's gone to her office to do just that."

"Good guess, Sherlock."

Reid glared at him. "She is not going to use herself as bait." He started walking towards the door.

"So did you?"

Reid gave him a confused look. "Did I?"

Brent smiled. "Kiss her in the closet."

Reid shrugged. "We're working with her."

"Yes, we are." Brent put his hands in his pocket and continued to look at him.

Reid stood there and looking at him for a few seconds then smirked as he turned, walking out the door. He ignored Brent's laughter. If he hurried, he could get to her office before she had time to do something stupid.

~

Jac opened the office door, difficult with Sandy almost pushing her through it. "I can't believe you're going to do this."

Jac walked in and flipped the lights on. "We're not getting anywhere, this might work."

Sandy dropped her bag on the table, and then tossed her jacket on top. "But you won't go out with any of them, without backup or whatever, *right?*"

Jac shook her head as she turned on the computer. "Do I look suicidal, Doctor?"

Sandy smirked. "No, no you don't." She dragged the chair around beside Jac's. "We can make you out to be some spoiled socialite? This is going to be fun." She rubbed her hands together and laughed. "I've never created a whole person before."

Jac laughed at her friend. "And you think I need to get out more?" They both leaned towards the screen as she typed in her username and password.

Reid sat there in his car scowling at the building. He'd gotten here in plenty of time. Enough time to see Jacinda flee from the taxi and look around excitedly. It didn't take him long to see what she was looking for, as her doctor friend quickly appeared from the parking area. They were both standing there; he could see Jac was filling the other woman in on the plan, and then they both looked excited. The blonde went from her cool doctor exterior to a conniving, grinning accomplice within a few seconds.

He gave them a few minutes to go upstairs and get started on the profile. Did she not understand what she was doing? He was not willing to go and identify her as victim number five at some crime scene. She was a hell of an investigator and that's where it stopped. She was not an undercover agent or bait, or going to be more involved in this, except from the safety of the basement office. He let out a long breath as he climbed out of his car. Making his way across the street, he ran up the steps to her building and yanked the door open. "Time's up, ladies."

Jac stood beside the desk as Sandy typed. "Those are my interests and hobbies?" She grinned as she went to the small refrigerator and pulled out two bottles of water. "I don't even know what a few of those are. Sandy, can't we at least tone it down a bit so if I have to reply to any messages, I know what I'm writing?"

Sandy laughed and pushed the chair back from the desk. Taking the bottle of water, she tapped the cap with a manicured fingernail. "You'll do fine. You don't have to be this person, just fake it for a while." She opened the cap then grinned at her across the desk. "So how rich are we going to make you?"

"I'd say dirt poor."

Jac jumped and turned towards the door with a little squeak.

Reid grinned at her. He peered around her at Sandy. "Ladies, I was in the neighborhood and thought I'd stop in and say hi."

Jac hoped he couldn't hear how fast her heart was beating. "We were just…"

"Being rebellious?" He offered as he walked around and looked at the computer screen. He grinned down at Sandy, who sat there looking guilty. "Doctor Gains."

Sandy gave him a little wave. Her eyes darted to Jac as she stood up slowly. "I should probably go."

Jac nodded but continued to stand, glaring at the man looking far too pleased with himself as he stood behind her desk.

They stood there silent and staring as Sandy picked up her coat and bag and slipped quietly out the door.

Reid sat down in her chair and studied the monitor. "You like skeet shooting?"

"Not particularly," she said through clenched teeth.

He leaned on the desk and looked at her. "What part of we don't use people as bait didn't you grasp?" His tone was oddly gentle.

"I wasn't going to use myself as bait." Her eyes studied the floor. "Not in a physical sense. I only…"

"Not in any sense." He stood up slowly to walk around the desk, coming to stand in front of her.

Jac flung her hands up in frustration. "I just want to find this person—this person that…" She stopped and took a deep breath. "It's so, so disgusting, to kill someone for a bit of money," She finished quietly.

"Yes." Reid stuffed his hands into his pockets and watched her. "Erase the profile, you're not publishing it."

Crossing her arms over her chest she looked up at him and chewed her lip. "I could just talk to them in the message area, maybe we could …"

"Erase it." His eyes were hard. He reached out as if he was going to place a hand on her shoulder.

Jac stepped back quickly, and moved behind her desk. Sitting down she began hitting the backspace button. She knew she was hitting it much harder than she needed to, but it stopped her from throwing something at him. When she had erased everything Sandy had typed, she motioned to the screen.

Reid came around behind the desk and scrolled down. He found the settings and clicked on 'change password'.

Her eyes bore into his back as he moved over and typed something. When he moved again, she could see the screen confirming the new password. *He'd locked her out of her own profile!*

Closing the screen, he straightened up and glanced down at her. She could feel the anger boiling through her veins while he stood there smirking. "Can I give you a ride home?" He stuffed his hands in his pockets, the expression in his eyes changing to something she couldn't quite determine.

Sandy would most likely be sitting down in the parking lot waiting to see what happened, so she shook her head.

Reid sighed and walked around the desk to the door. "I'll see you in the morning." He paused and looked like he wanted to say something more. "Have a good night." He stepped out the door quickly.

11

Reid bolted upright when his phone rang. He grasped at the table a few times before he opened his eyes and squinted at the clock. Three o'clock? He fumbled the phone to his ear. "Lo?"

"There's a fifth one."

His whole body was suddenly awake and alert. "Fuck. Where?" He leaned over, flipping on the light and grabbed the pen. Brent mumbled the address. "Want me to pick you up?" He rubbed a hand over his eyes as he nodded. "Be there in fifteen." Hanging up, he sat there for a moment. A fifth? "Fuck!" He'd really wanted to think it was over when the account was closed.

Standing up, he squinted and looked around for his stuff. Shaking his head in a futile attempt to get coherent, he opened the closet. They had to find a way to stop this one. Pulling his jeans on he stumbled over to grab a shirt. Hopefully with Jacinda's help they could trace things before the trail got cold.

He paused while pulling on his boots and realized what he was thinking. He couldn't wake her at this hour. He pulled on the second boot and then stood before going over to pick up his cell phone and unplug the charger.

Shaking his head, he grabbed his keys. The second they had the scene recorded, he'd get her down at the station to work her magic on the computer.

~

Jac hit the alarm again, but the ringing didn't stop. Opening her eyes, she frowned at the clock. It wasn't time to get up yet. The phone? The phone was ringing. Flopping to the other side of the bed she grabbed it. "Hello?"

"Sorry to wake you. It's Reid."

She bolted upright. "What's wrong?" Her heart was beating so loudly in her ears she worried she wouldn't hear his answer.

"Can you come in now?"

She looked at the clock; the little hand was on the five… Putting her hand on her chest she took a breath. "There's another one," she whispered.

"Yes."

Kicking the covers back, she slid to the side of the bed. "I'll grab a cab and be there as soon as possible."

"I'm already headed your way."

"Oh. I'll see you shortly then."

"Yep." He hung up.

It seemed like she had just hung up the phone when someone knocked on her door. She only had her jeans on so far. Grabbing a sweater, she pulled it on and held it close as she went to the door.

He just stood there for a moment, his eyes traveling over the length of her before he stepped through the open doorway. "Sorry about the time." His eyes moved over her hair several times, and she wondered if it was standing on end.

Jac waved him in. "It's fine. Come in," She closed the door. "Just let me find a top and I'll be ready to go." She quickly walked to her room, figuring it was too early in the morning to wonder what the look on his face meant.

Pulling a sweatshirt over her top, she paused when she stepped back into the room. "Is it the same?"

Reid nodded. "So far."

Picking up her cell phone she stuffed it into her purse, and then looked over at him. "Do you know who she is?"

He shook his head. "Brent is at the station right now." He stood there with his hand on the doorknob watching her pull her shoes on. "We're hoping if we can get the financial data as soon as the banks open, we may be able to be waiting when the money is picked up."

Jacinda straightened and nodded. Sighing, she rubbed a hand against her forehead. "I'd hoped…"

"We all did."

"I'm ready, let's go."

Jac sat beside him during the silent ride to the station. She didn't know if she could walk into a building where the body was found. The number of people on the scene meant that vibes would be on everything.

Reid kept glancing at her, but she couldn't make small talk right now. He reached over and lightly gripped her hand. "Thanks for understanding why we brought you in on this as quickly as possible."

She could feel his concern for her rush into her system, but there was something else she couldn't grasp. Then the first flash hit her, she took a deep breath. The cold backlash from being near death washed through her. Pulling her hand away quickly, she opened the window a crack and turned her face towards it. Taking deep breaths, she focused through the nausea. Glancing back over at him, she faked a yawn. "Trying to get my brain to kick in."

He grinned. "Tell me about it. Brent woke me at three and I wasn't even sure I had my boots on the right feet until about twenty minutes ago."

"Your job sucks," she said trying to sound more light-hearted than she felt.

He nodded. "At this time of day, all jobs suck."

She nodded and turned her face back towards the open window.

Brent looked over at them as they walked in. "Did he at least buy you coffee?"

She shook her head and went over to the computer. "Do you have a name?" Sitting down she switched on the computer.

"Just waiting on the call. The Captain is up there making sure it's done now. Everyone upstairs is either going over the scene again or pacing as they wait on reports." He stood up and picked up his cup. "I'll go harass them again and bring back coffee."

"Thank you." She looked over to see Reid staring at the board. "Was anything found with her?" He shook his head. Turning her focus back on the computer, she sat there in the silence.

She turned when she heard boots on the stairs a few minutes later. Brent came through the door with two cups and a piece of paper.

Setting his cup down as he walked by the round table, he handed Jac a cup then returned to pick up the marker and write on the board.

Jac had typed the name on the keyboard by the time he finished writing. Dawn Thomas, she hit enter. The name sounded vaguely familiar, but at this time of the morning, she couldn't focus enough to determine why. As the first search engine started, she opened another and quickly typed in the name. Picking up her cup she took a sip before she started with the third search.

Sitting back, she watched the search engines work. When a tear rolled down her cheek, she quickly wiped it away before anyone noticed. Taking another sip, she frowned and set her cup down. "How long until we have a credit card statement?" She asked without turning around.

"Can't get it until the office opens," Brent responded, sounding as defeated as she felt.

She stood up and looked back at the monitor. Glancing at the clock, she realized it had only been twenty minutes. As she went to turn away the first search stopped. Leaning down, she quickly clicked on it. Opening the page she read through it. Squinting at the screen she moved over to pick up the printout Brent had brought downstairs with the coffee. Same neighborhood. She went back over to the computer and printed out the article.

Both men were looking at her when she turned around from the computer. She went over to the board and wrote the information from the search engine. She set the marker down then went over and handed Brent the pages.

Reid watched her sit down at the computer, then looked at the board. Wealthy designer. Was what she had written. He took the paper Brent held out to him and scanned it quickly. When the printer started, he looked back at Brent, the same puzzled look on his face when they both turned to Jac.

Jac checked to make sure the search was ongoing before

spinning around to face the two men, confusion evident on their faces. "Apparently my brain works better when it's half asleep." She shrugged and walked over and held out the page. "Ms. Thomas has recently invested in several online businesses."

Reid frowned and looked at the page again. He frowned over at her. "I didn't find out much about the dating site, other than the address." She held up a finger and looked over at the printer as it finished a page. She walked over and picked it up.

"Ms. Thomas has recently invested large amounts of her time and fortune into several online firms, blah, blah, several smaller sites such as Web Clinic, Pen Palz, and Love Quest, under the guidance and expertise of designers from WebFix, these firms have been an instant success and Ms. Thomas believes it's only the beginning of, blah, blah." She stopped and shrugged. "Could be another dead end, but I found it interesting that a victim we've linked to the website also helped get it going."

Brent walked over and took the sheet of paper from her. "It's interesting all right."

She grinned. "I'm running a search on WebFix right now."

Reid grinned at her. "No more coffee for her, she's making us look like amateurs again."

Brent winked at her as he handed Reid the article. "What time does the Love Quest office open?"

"Nine." Jac glanced at the clock and sighed.

~

By nine, Jac was drooping over her desk. She'd run out of things to search almost an hour ago and had been killing time until the offices of Love Quest opened. Hopefully, she could convince Mrs. Oster to send her the confidential files.

Brent leaned over to look at her. "Still with us?" She nodded. "We're going up to talk to the Captain, can we bring you back something?"

She yawned. "I'll take a nap or a danish, whichever is the easiest." Brent chuckled as walked out the door behind his partner. Sighing she picked up the phone. Please let her still believe me.

When they walked back in, she was leaning against Brent's

desk. Reid looked at the board to see Love Quest written under the other information. He raised his eyebrows.

She shrugged. "I didn't feel like waiting for a credit card statements." She waved a few pieces of paper. "I have Dawn's list from Love Quest."

Brent set a bottle of juice and a danish on the desk. "You already cross-referenced the Love Quests list too?" He shook his head then winked at her. "You're slacking."

Jac smiled at him sweetly. "Oh, I've cross-referenced already, none of them are the same as the other four." She tossed the list on the table to join the scattered pieces of paper. Sighing, she picked up the bottle of juice. "I've run out of ideas or plans." She glared at Reid. "That I'm *allowed* to do."

Brent gave him a look, and then studied the papers scattered over the table. "So, we wait for the video and the financial statement."

Reid dropped down into his chair and ran a hand through his hair until it was standing on end. "Shit." He watched her recognizing that she felt crushed by the possibility that they weren't going to get the person responsible. His expression softened for a brief second before he cleared his throat and glanced at the clock. "Let's go get some breakfast."

~

Jac stood between the two men and they all stared at the screen. She'd lost count how many times the video had been rewound and slowly played through. Checking the time of the transfer, she studied the screen one more time. "Do you think if it were enlarged it we could see more?"

Reid rubbed his temple in thought. "I doubt it, it's already blurry."

"Are those sunglasses or those tinted things?" Brent asked quietly.

Jac turned her head again and squinted at the image frozen on the screen. "I'm going to go with sunglasses, reading glasses that size went out in the seventies." Sighing she wandered back over to the board. "I'm almost out of ideas."

Reid turned and looked at her. "Almost? Does that mean you have more?" He tossed the financial printouts on the table. "I'm out. Ms. Thomas hasn't transferred any large amounts, hasn't charged any strange things." He pinched the bridge of his nose. "We can't get more details on her finances until the judge probates the estate, which could take weeks." He looked at Brent. "The post office boxes tied to the closed bank account, as well as the identification used to pick up the wire transfer are dead ends, because the boxes are no longer in use." Stuffing his hands in his pockets he shrugged. "Somehow the blood toxicology results were botched up, so we wait for those, again. Not that it matters, nothing unusual was found in the other victims' blood screens."

Brent walked over and sat in the first chair he came to. "We're missing something here. Something that is sitting right in front of our faces."

Jac chewed her lip and looked at the board again. She had an idea, but how could she persuade them to let her try it? Telling them the truth would just get her escorted from the building or sent home to nap. Picking up the marker she went to the left end of the board.

"Where was Clair found?" She gave Brent a tired look. "I know it's in the files, but my brain isn't at its best at the moment."

Reid leaned against the desk and shrugged. "Empty parking lot, middle of nowhere." He watched her write it on the board. "Between two buildings in an old neighborhood", She nodded as she wrote and stepped over to the third one quickly. "In a park." He didn't need to tell her the last two; she quickly wrote them on the board.

Setting the marker down she backed up and looked at the board. Come on, think of a way to lead into this discussion. "Have you put these on a map? Is there some sort of pattern?" Now you're just sad - grasping at ideas from movies.

Brent gave Reid a puzzled look, shrugging Brent got up to get a map of the area. It took him a few minutes to write the victim's numbers on the map, then stood back and watched Jac lean over and study it silently.

Jac chewed her lip again. Now or never. Sighing, she turned around to face them again. "I'd like to go look at the sites."

Brent's eyebrows shot up, but he didn't comment.

Reid continued to lean against the desk and study her. "I don't see how that would help."

She paced over to the board. "I don't see how, at this point, it could hurt either." She threw up her hands as she turned to look at them. "I need a new perspective, and then maybe I will come up with something. I think Brent's right and we've been walking right by some important detail and not paying attention."

Reid studied her quietly. He was scowling or squinting at her, she wasn't sure, but if she guessed, he knew she was hiding something. He straightened off the desk. "I don't understand what you think you'll find at the crime scenes." He looked at Brent who shrugged and sent him a blank look. "We went over them dozens of times, our team went over them. More than a month has passed for the first one…"

Jac threw her hands up then dropped them to her hips. "I know. I'm not saying you missed anything." She walked over and looked up out of the tiny window. "I do know I've checked every idea, cross-referenced every possible combination and if we all sit here much longer staring at computers or the board, we're going to go insane." She walked back over and tapped the folders and papers scattered all over the table. "In these, we found nothing, the victims were in immaculately clean clothes, which still leaves a question of how can that be? But that's it, nothing more, anywhere." She chewed the inside of her lip again. Other than paper, clothes were things that held no memories. She just needed one solid glimpse then maybe she could take this idea and lead them somewhere.

Brent leaned back in the chair he'd dropped into and crossed his arms. He looked amused as he watched his partner. Reid was less than impressed with her suggestion, the closed look on his face gave that away. He focused on the board and then turned his gaze to her again.

She stood there, chewing her lip with her hands on her hips and dropped her eyes to study the floor. She glanced up to see Reid glaring, as if he was trying to figure it out. Something flashed quickly over his face, but it was gone so fast she didn't have time to decide what he could be thinking. Her heart ached to be able to tell them something, *anything* that would make them let her go to the scenes and use what she could to find justice for those poor women.

He flung a hand up. "Just tell me why," he said, his eyes searching her face.

Jac hesitated for a moment. I *wish I could.* If I could just see where his thoughts were… She moved, almost involuntarily toward him, coming to a stop less than a foot in front of him and placed a hand on the arms he had crossed in front of his heart.

His eyes said he was furious, but his emotions were torn between wanting to help and wanting to walk away. Good, she thought without smiling. Indecision I can work with. "Please, Reid, just take me and let me look." She dropped her hand from his arm. "I will explain everything, after, if there's anything to explain."

He was shocked she had finally said his name. He was more shocked he was going to agree. He looked down into her pleading, sleepy eyes. "Fine." He turned abruptly before he said something stupid and walked out of the office.

Brent sat there without moving. Huh, the mighty Reid has a weakness after all, and it comes in the form of soft brown eyes. He smirked for a moment and then looked over at Jac. "Better hurry or he'll leave us both here."

She grinned and quickly grabbed her purse.

12

Jac looked around the empty parking lot. It wasn't clear why anyone would ever need to be here. She glanced back at the two men sitting in the car. *They're going to think you're crazy.* She turned and walked over to the spot that had been pointed out to her.

It wouldn't be the first time someone thought she was crazy, she frowned at the broken asphalt, it probably wouldn't be the last.

Taking a deep breath, she knelt and placed both hands on the ground. There were vibrations, faint but there. She focused harder, nothing was solid enough to grab. Moving her hands slowly, to try a few more places.

"What is she doing?" Reid growled.

Brent shrugged. "I'm not sure." He looked over in the direction she was looking. "Does she see something?"

Reid frowned. "Maybe."

Brent looked away from her and studied his partner. "Why, exactly, are we doing this again?"

Reid rubbed his forehead quickly, and then glanced back to her. "Because we're out of ideas, and she has looked at the same things we've looked at all along and then come up with something to follow. Every time."

Brent nodded and turned back to watch Jac. "She's presently looking at an empty lot, surrounded by nothing, pretty sure she's seeing the same things we did." She was walking slowly back towards them. "Why do we have to wait in the car?"

Reid shook his head. "I don't know."

Both men swung around in their seat to look at her when she got in the back seat. She smiled. "Next."

Brent snorted at Reid as he turned back around.

~

She knew they were both aggravated with her as she climbed out of the car at the third site. The second one had been between two buildings, and again there was nothing for her to pick up energy from.

Stopping in front of the bench she looked at it before making sure no one else was in the little park.

Walking behind the bench, she glanced over at the car holding the two detectives waiting for her. "Please." She whispered to herself. "Just see something."

Placing her hands on the back of the bench she turned away from the watching men. She smirked as the vibrations from two amorous teens flew through her mind. Moving slowly, she ran her hands across the wood towards the end of the bench.

Breathing slowly, she scanned as she went; there it was—a vibration on this bench that wasn't quite right. She had to pinpoint the spot where it was strong enough to drown out everything that came after. She frowned as she concentrated, there it was. Just a bit of anger.

Frowning again, she walked around to sit on the bench, placing her hands beside her. Come on, one glimpse, that's all she would need to grasp at the images filtering through her mind. Again, she had to sift through the layers of time, until she sensed a fear so intense every nerve in her body jumped at the same moment.

Jac could feel the struggle and panic. Turning her head, she closed her eyes so she could see clearly. Willing her mind to let it come through, she took several slow steady breaths. This was the spot she had been looking for. The emotions were intense, consuming but not evil. She began to absorb the emotions and visions that were present in the vibrations.

Her stomach tightened, as it always did, when she subjected herself to absorbing emotions. Jac fought against the faint tremor in her muscles and forced her body to relax and let things happen.

"Is she taking a break, or thinking or what?"

Reid snapped his head around to look over at his partner. "How the hell should I know? I'm still wondering why we have to sit in the car."

Brent frowned and looked back at Jac. She was still sitting on the bench looking at a building on the outskirts of the park. At least he thought that was what she was staring at.

Both men jumped when she suddenly looked straight up, bolting up off the bench. She stood looking at the same building holding her hand over her stomach.

Reid's hand was on the door handle ready to rush over when she turned and took a few slow steps towards them. Her head came up and she started sprinting to the car.

Climbing in the back she huffed out a breath, "Quickly, let's get to the next one before this is gone."

Brent watched Reid turn without question and start the car. Reid wondered if his partner was thinking the same things he was. Once again, she'd thought of an angle they hadn't. Jacinda would be dynamite if she ever had any investigative training.

He glanced in the mirror for the tenth time. She just sat there with a faraway look on her face.

When they pulled up to the empty factory Reid opened his door. "I'll show you where to go."

Jac climbed out of the car and shook her head. "No, stay here, I read the report." She walked, almost swaying, over to the door hanging open with no latch of any kind, and stepped inside.

Brent climbed out of the car and looked across the roof at his stewing friend. "I don't think it's safe for…"

Reid nodded. "I know, that's why I'm listening in case she runs into trouble." He looked at his partner, and then turned and started to walk towards the building.

Brent followed him, giving him a puzzled look when he stopped outside the door she'd gone in.

Both stood there in the silence and listened.

Jac found the location without issue. Remnants of the yellow police tape were still hanging. Standing there for a moment she looked down at the faded marks on the floor. How did he kill these women, yet their clothes were without a wrinkle? Why did her mind keep going back to that?

Walking over she knelt where the few chalk outlines remained. Taking a deep breath, she placed both hands on the dusty board floor. A wave of nausea hit her so fast; she lifted her hands to her chest and took a few breaths to steady herself. Slowly, she opened her hands and placed them on the floor again. The killer had touched this part of the floor. Swallowing the bile in her throat, she quickly moved over further, hoping she didn't contact the killer's thoughts again. The suffering she would go through to find out who had done this was for the women, the victims, she wasn't sure if she would be able to climb back to the surface if she absorbed a murderer's inner emotions.

Taking a deep breath, she placed her hands on the floor again. When the black swirled through her, she fought against it and reached deeper. Jac could feel Elaine's desperation, the panic engulfing her as she struggled to do something, anything, to free herself. She saw a hand move towards her again.

The panic and fear began to fade as acceptance took over.

Jac closed her eyes and lifted her face towards the ceiling as she felt the other woman's emotions: fear, revulsion and a strange acceptance flood into her. Jac's stomach fought violently against the sensations. Steadying her breathing, she knew the headache that always came wasn't far off. Her own determination to finish this was the only thing that kept her kneeling there.

They heard her footsteps moving quickly towards them. With one hand on his gun, Reid pulled the door open further as he looked in cautiously.

Brent had stepped back to get a clear view of whatever came out of the door.

Jac ran through it, almost running into them. She stopped in front of Reid, gripping her stomach. "We have to hurry. If I lose this, I can't do *that* again." She turned, heading quickly to the car.

"Lose what?" He called after her.

When Reid climbed in the car and looked at her, he was determined to get answers. Her face was pale, she was shaking. She was holding her head and squeezing her eyes closed. When she turned and looked at him with a plea in her eyes, he hesitated.

"I'll tell you everything, soon, we have to hurry," she

whispered.

Brent rubbed the back of his neck, as he looked at him

Reid looked in the mirror. She really didn't look well. "As soon as you look at this last one, you better tell me something or I'm going to get really pissed."

Her empty eyes didn't meet his in the mirror, but she nodded.

When the car stopped at the dock, she almost asked to keep going. She knew this site would hold stronger emotions than the others, since very little time had passed since the murder happened. She also knew it might give her a very clear image of the killer and that reason alone made her body move to get out of the car.

Every muscle in her body was threatening to quit on her. She had to concentrate on her breathing to keep her stomach under control. Carefully, Jac walked over the rocky ground that led down towards the old dock that seemed oddly out of place in today's modern world of cement. A small wooden boat sat under it, in the shadows of the faded planks. Taking a deep breath, she looked around to see if they were alone. She could see no one.

Walking out onto the swaying dock, she stood above the small boat. Staring down into it, she willed herself to take the steps and move toward it. She looked out into the water for a moment, and then dug deep to find the courage she needed. It was buried under the queasiness from the emotions her visions had brought. She had never intentionally tried to see this much at one time before; fear gripped her when she realized she wasn't sure of the outcome. Would she be able to stay conscious through it?

Nodding to no one, she turned and walked off the dock, heading to the small boat in the overgrowth of shoreline weeds, long forgotten in today's world of metal and motors. Stopping, she looked at the reeds that were bent over, broken and dying. She couldn't look back at the detectives waiting for her in the car. If she did, she would lose her nerve and would never come back.

Jac wished she wasn't in plain view of the men but knew she had pushed her luck as far as she could with them. She would have to do this in front of them. Please don't do anything embarrassing, she begged herself silently.

To steady herself, she grasped a large support beam. Dropping her hand, she gasped. A flash of anger washed through her. She stood there for a moment, trying to feel what was behind the dark emotion. It was too scattered and unfocused.

Breathing slowly, she bent down and climbed into the boat. She slowly lowered herself and sat, only touching the gunwale at the top to steady her. The vibrations were humming through her arms; she knew this was going to hit her harder than anything ever had before. She'd encountered dark emotions before, but this was going to be like nothing she'd ever experienced.

Keeping her breathing steady, she closed her eyes and braced herself for whatever she was going to see. Lowering her hands, an inch at a time, she touched the floor of the rotting craft. She held her head high; needing to feel the clear air brushing against her face gently.

A feeling of grogginess was first, a lethargic sensation she hadn't felt from the others. Had Dawn Thomas been drugged? Show me, she silently asked the woman no longer physically in this world.

Shock flooded into her; she could feel her fighting against the groggy weight taking over her body. Jac glimpsed a flash of a jacket or shirt, before another moment of darkness.

Focusing, she breathed through the pounding that started in her head, as she ran her hands further over the floorboards. If she could just find that *one* clear moment.

She felt the veil of fog lifting from Dawn, the realization that this was really happening. Sluggishness changed to anger so quickly she jolted but forced her hands to stay on the wood.

Feelings of utter shock, then more anger filled her mind. Shaking her head slightly she watched and waited. Her heart sped up; she could feel it beating through her whole body as a burst of strength from the victim's spirit enveloped her.

Folding herself forward Jac fought against her body's desire to escape into unconsciousness, threatening to overtake her. You can't pass out now, she told herself. Pushing her hands harder against the wood, she grit her teeth in determination.

Reid leaned closer to the windshield watching at her. He sensed Brent was also leaning forward trying to see better. "I don't think, something is…" He was out the door the second she flipped out of the boat landing sprawled on the ground beside it.

He heard Brent behind him, as he raced down the worn pathway leading to the dock. She was trying to get to her feet, scrambling along on her hands and knees still heading towards them.

Kneeling on the stones, she rested her forehead in her hands for a moment. The cool stones beneath her cheek helped her to focus. Trying to stay conscious she fought the waves of nausea that were almost drowning her. She could hear the footsteps advancing towards her on the loose stones. *Get it together before they get here.*

Pushing herself up onto her hands and knees, she leaned slowly back trying to breathe through the dizziness. Opening her eyes, she concentrated on bringing the men into focus. Up you get now. Everything was blurry and shaking. Pushing against her knees, she managed to be close to upright. Bending over, resting a hand on the cool stones, she held up her other hand towards them. They were a few feet from her. "Don't touch me." She gasped, trying to say it as loud as she could. Squinting, she saw both men's feet beside her. Dropping her head, she took a few more deep breaths. "Happens all the time."

Reid shifted on the loose stones and leaned down. "What happens?" She could hear the panic in his voice.

Jac shook her head trying to clear the haze. "I need to get home." She tried to straighten up but dropped back down to lean on her knees. Fumbling for her pocket, she pulled out her phone, promptly dropping it on the rocks. Opening her eyes again she watched Reid squat down, studying her face. The concern in his eyes almost made her cry. History reminded her that he would lose that look when he learned the truth.

"Jacinda." He hissed out a breath. "Let us help you get to the car."

Jac could barely manage to shake her head; at least she was pretty sure she shook it. "Can …" She took another breath; the nauseas feeling was almost more than she could bear. "Call Sandy, press one." She moved slowly into a squatting, half-kneeling position, holding her own thighs to keep her head and shoulders upright. Her muscles were shaking and so weak, she wasn't sure how much longer she would be able to hold herself up.

Reid silently flipped her phone open and pushed the button. Putting out her hand he set the phone in her palm. With a shaking arm, she held the phone to her ear. The second she heard her voice, she almost cried. Sandy, the only person, since her mother, that would help her. "Sand—need—home…"

Reid could hear the woman's voice on the other end.

"Jac? Where are you? Are you alone? Jac…"

"Detectives," Jac whispered into the phone.

"Give him the phone. Jac? Stay focused and give him the phone before you pass out on me!"

Jac leaned down onto her legs further and moved the phone in the direction Reid was in. "Talk." She panted to him.

Reid took the phone, hesitantly putting it to his ear. "Doctor?" She began barking orders so quickly, yelling into the phone because even in her present state, Jac could still hear her.

"Has she passed out yet? She should have smelling salts in her purse. Use them. Get her home now! I'll meet you there. Don't touch her if you can help it, it only makes it harder for her."

He paused for a second and looked at her, he seemed blurry through her eyes right now. "We'll meet you there." He abruptly hung up the phone. Stuffing it quickly into his pocket, he turned to the man beside him. "She has salts or something in her purse."

Brent turned and ran back up the incline to the car.

Reid reached out to touch her, and then dropped his hand down onto the rocks so he could lean closer to her. "Jacinda, let me help." She didn't reply just kept breathing very loudly. He didn't know why she would pass out, but if she carried salts with her then it meant that passing out was bad. "Talk to me, can you hear me?" He wanted to brush the long hair off her face, but didn't, because he still wasn't sure why he shouldn't touch her. "Stay with me, Brent has gone to get your purse."

"I'm not a freak." She said it breathlessly.

Confused he shook his head. "Only freak here is me *freaking* out, honey, just stay with me, we'll get you home shortly." He turned when he heard Brent sliding down to kneel beside him. Grabbing the purse, he dug through it. Why was it when a man put his hand in a woman's purse he felt like he was violating some sacred space? Unable to tell one thing from the other that he touched, he leaned back down to her. "What am I looking for here?"

If she hadn't wanted to throw up, she might find the uncertainty in his voice amusing. "Black case."

He nodded pulling out a few more things. He finally pulled out a black case; dropping the purse he opened it quickly. The smell must have hit him because he made a weird face before he held it in the vicinity of her face.

Jac gasped, and then turned her head toward it and inhaled a few times. Taking a few shaky breaths, she lifted her head. She couldn't bring herself to make eye contact. If she did, she might start crying to see the concern she knew would change to abhorrence soon enough. "I don't know how long—that will work." She tried again with shaky arms to push herself up further. "Have to get to Sandy." She whispered and chanced a glance at them.

"I'll carry you," Brent said as he stood quickly.

Reid shook his head quickly at him. "Touching her will only make it worse." Brent shot him a look of confusion. Reid shrugged. "I don't know either."

Jac felt sorrier for them than she did herself. Here were two big guys, used to just taking over, and now they stood here feeling helpless for, most likely, the first time in their lives. "Don't touch my skin, just get me standing please."

She heard both men scramble on the stone, moving to behind her. Big hands grasped under her arms and had her on her feet before she could have gotten there on her own, even in a normal state. She felt the hands hesitantly let her go. Nodding she stood there for a moment, breathing shallowly. Looking at the loose rock, then the distance to the car, she tried to move her foot. "Just don't let me fall and break my face on those." She wobbled on the first step, reaching out quickly to grasp Reid's sleeve. Weakness filled her head again; she knew then she couldn't walk this uneven ground on her own accord.

Hanging onto his sleeve she looked up at the worried eyes studying her. Her stomach still churned from the emotions she'd drawn in. She blinked as a tear rolled down her cheek. "I'm not going to make it up there, Reid…" She felt her knees give out a bit and gripped his shirt harder.

Reid stood there looking down at the pale woman. Her eyes were begging him to help her. When they filled with tears he wanted to scream 'how'? Glancing quickly at his partner he knew if he didn't pick her up and take the chance his partner was one second from doing it. "Get the door open." He growled as he bent down, quickly scooping her into his arms. He resisted the urge to push her face into his neck as he moved quickly up the hill.

Brent, two steps ahead of him and had the back door held open. As he put her gently into the back seat, he saw his partner flinging her purse in and climb into the drivers' seat.

"I'm driving. You'll get us all killed."

He heard him mumble as he shut the door. Reid looked at her again, she was leaning with her head back, eyes closed hugging the black case against her chest. Brent was right. He closed the door and ran around to the passenger side, climbing in the back beside her.

13

Getting Jacinda from the car into her small house, without touching her too much, was a challenge, but they managed.

Both men were standing there looking at her stretched out on her couch, when the door flew open as Doctor Gains ran over to her.

Sandy knelt down beside the couch, brushing the hair off Jac's face. "Oh, look at you. What did you do this time?" Jac didn't respond; just lay there with her eyes closed, breathing slowly. She stood up and started for the kitchen. "What was she doing?" She glared at the men as she passed.

Reid followed her to the kitchen, stopping where he could still see the couch. "What medical condition does she have?"

Sandy turned, setting the canister on the counter. "I wish this was a medical condition that could be cured." She grabbed the kettle and filled it. Plugging it in, she opened another cupboard. "Now tell me, what was she doing?"

Reid's mind was swimming. A medical condition that had no cure? She couldn't be cured? "Uh, she wanted to go to the sites and look around…" The woman spun around to glare at him.

"The murder sites? Where bodies were found?" The tall man nodded, she slammed the box onto the counter and then ran to Jac. Dropping to her knees she leaned right over her face. "You were playing in death?" She brushed the hair away from her pale friends face again. "Are you crazy? Do you want to be a vegetable or something? We don't know what could happen, you were practically paralyzed the last…"

Jac's mouth quivered. "You're losin' your cool in front of the men, doctor."

"Oh, who cares." Sandy dropped back onto her heels and looked at her. "What am I going to do with you?"

Jacinda opened her eyes slowly, turning her head. "Make me tea?"

Sandy scowled at her. "You'll be lucky if I don't pour it over your head!" Standing up, she walked back to the kitchen shaking her head.

"I'll have the detectives arrest you if you do…" Jac called softly after her. She saw Brent standing at her feet looking down. She knew Reid was behind her, looking more confused than his partner. "Oh, inquisition time, I hate this part." She pouted at Brent. "Just give me a few minutes and I'll explain everything." Turning, she looked up at the green eyes studying her face. "*Completely.*" She whispered.

She continued to look up at Reid. He felt like she was asking him to find patience and understanding, but his mind was so mixed up right now, he didn't know what he was supposed to think. Moving slowly, he leaned down on the back of the couch and looked into the pained brown eyes. "You scared the shit out of us."

She bit her lip. "Sorry."

Reid sighed. "Just do what you have to do; we'll discuss this, in detail, later."

Jac nodded, closing her eyes for a few seconds, she blew out a breath. Her head was a blend of pain and spinning at this point. She knew she had very little time before sleep took her, she had to try to explain. Opening her eyes, she was surprised to see Reid's face still hovering over hers. "Did they check the blood screens again?" His eyes widened. "I think Ms. Thomas was possibly drugged, or drunk or something." She glanced away from the serious green eyes to the man standing at her feet. "And I think we need to find out if any of the women—had suitcases packed—even overnight bags." Jac didn't like the blank expression on Brent's face so she looked slowly back to Reid. His wasn't much better. Taking a few more deep breaths, she tried again. "I think maybe the change of clothes was done after the murder."

"No shop talk until you can sit up." Sandy walked over carrying a tray. "Get yourself propped up and get this into you."

Jac knew Sandy's voice sounded harsh, but she also knew that if she looked at her friend's face, she would see concern, if not tears. "Yes, doctor." She mocked, pulling herself slowly up on the cushions. With a shaky hand, she clasped the cup Sandy held in front of her. She hated this part too. "Uh, can't they make this stuff smell better?" She grimaced, then sighed before taking the first sip.

Sandy sat on the edge of the coffee table, looking at the men still towering over her. "Sit! Let her at least settle her stomach before you start grilling her."

Jac moved only her eyes to look at Reid. He was looking at Sandy, with his eyes huge. "Doctor, we don't even know where to start."

Sandy smirked as the men moved to sit. "I'm warning you, the first obscenity or foul name you use, I'll have you removed from this building so fast you won't know what happened."

Jac gave her a shocked look. "Wow, did you get up on the wrong side of the bed today or what?"

Sandy covered her face for a moment and took a few breaths. "You scare me to death every time, Jac." She dropped her hands into her lap. "I've been so afraid you would try something like this, as soon as you told me what you were doing." She shook her head. "I know you want to help but…"

"There was no other option, Sandy, they found another last night. We've hit walls in all directions…"

Sandy held up her hand, studying her for a moment. "Last night?" Sandy moved quickly to sit beside her. "You're lucky you didn't put yourself into a coma."

Jac kept her head down; trying to avoid eye contact with the men.

Brent leaned forward on the chair. "I know we're detectives and puzzles are kind of what we do, but if you two don't explain soon, my brain is going to implode."

Jac grinned at him and then covered her face. She sipped the tea again, an obvious stalling tactic. Hesitating, she glanced over at Reid. He sat opposite her, leaning forward on his knees, watching and waiting. "It's not that I don't want to explain, I just don't know *how* to explain." Slowly, she sat up and waited for her head to stop spinning. Exhaling loudly, she looked from one man to the other. "Every time I've tried to explain, it hasn't gone well."

Sandy sat there, watching her intently. Sandy knew what she could do, but from the look on her face, she didn't know how to explain it either. Turning her head, she looked at the men briefly and then back to Jac. "You could do what you did with me, I mean, once I stopped freaking out, I was okay."

Jac smirked at her. "Freaking out? I thought you were going to beat me to death with your black vase."

Sandy shrugged. "Reflex. What we don't understand scares us, so we tend to want to squash it."

Reid sighed. "Someone—anyone, explain *something*." He glanced at Brent briefly. "I am not a patient man." He held up his hand with his thumb and first finger an inch apart. "I have about this much left before I start growling."

Sandy smirked at his demonstration. She glanced at Jac, who sighed in defeat, knowing she couldn't delay what she hesitated to do in the first place. Looking back at the two men, Sandy leaned forward taking on her doctor's persona. "Jacinda can sometimes see things." Both men continued to stare at her blankly. She turned back Jac, who rolled her eyes and sighed loudly.

"Fine." Pushing herself up, she turned around until her back was facing them. Leaning against the couch she mumbled. "I feel like I'm in some freaky magic show when I do this, Sandy."

Sandy bit her lip to hide her grin, and then looked back at the men. "By See, I mean see images and things, but not with her eyes." She ignored the skeptical snort that came from one of the men, but her spine straightened. "I'll need something personal from each of you, but not embarrassing, please." Sandy stood up and held her hand out towards Brent. He didn't move. She pushed her open hand more aggressively toward him. "This is not a ploy. Do you want answers or not?"

Brent just sat there and looked at her. Reid stifled a sigh. They were pulling his leg, right? This was a joke of some kind. When Sandy continued to stand there, without so much as a smirk, he frowned over at his partner. Reid shook his head in disbelief.

"It can't be paper or clothing," Jac said quietly.

Brent reached into his shirt, pulling out his chain and pendant. Lifting it over his head, he handed it to the crazy woman standing there, impatiently holding out her hand.

Reid gave her a "you've got to be kidding" look when she stepped in front of him. When she continued to stand there, glaring at him, he leaned back and pulled his keys out of his pocket. Working the pendant off the ring, he handed it to her and leaned back again. He knew his blood pressure was going to spike if they didn't stop screwing around, then he would start yelling.

Sandy sat down behind Jac. "Ready?"

"Yeah." Jac held up her hand, palm up. When the doctor lowered Brent's chain into it, Jac closed her hand around it and took a few deep breaths, as if she was trying to find some focus.

He knew Brent was waiting for them to say, 'gotcha!' as he was. When he heard Jac laugh softly, he figured it was now.

Jac shook her head. "Really Sandy, next time please specify something they weren't wearing during sex." She smirked. "Cute blonde though Brent, love the ladybug tattoo."

He leaned forward and squinted at her. The doctor looked over a Brent with a smug look on her face. She turned back towards Jac when she heard her sigh again.

"Your mom gave this to you when you graduated from the academy, that's so sweet that you wear it, Brent."

Reid's head snapped around to see the look of complete shock on his partner's face. He didn't know how she knew, but he knew from his friend's expression she couldn't have been more on target.

Carefully, the doctor took the necklace out of Jac's open hand and reached over and held it out to his still shocked looking partner. She waited while Jac took a sip of her tea. "Are you okay?"

Jac shrugged. "Weak as a baby. My head is starting to pound, I'm still not sure I won't pass out or throw up, but I've got enough left in me to finish this."

Sandy looked at her opened palm again, and then lowered the small angel pendant from Reid into it.

Jac closed her hand. She took a deep breath, then smiled. "This little angel has seen a lot of miles and moods, Reid." He frowned. Anyone would know he drove a lot of miles, it was part of his job.

She opened her eyes suddenly and looked at him. "I'm shocked," she whispered. Closing her eyes again, she cocked her head to the side a bit. "The sister must have thought you'd need your own personal guardian angel throughout your life. Reid, it's sadly touching." Holding up her hand, she waited for her friend to take the pendant back. "I just need a few minutes here."

Sandy leaned over and held the angel out to him.

He scowled at her and took it from her hand. Reid went over to the window. How did she know that? No one on the planet knew that, but himself and Sister Mary.

Jac opened her eyes and looked at Sandy as she stared at the tension radiating off the man standing by the window, and then Brent, who still hadn't closed his gaping mouth. "This moment, gentlemen, is where my warning comes into effect," Sandy said very loudly and sternly. Rubbing a hand over Jac's shoulder, "Do you want to try more tea or something light to eat now?" She glanced at the clock. "You know you're going to take a really long nap shortly. It always goes better if you have something in your system."

Jac just nodded but continued to lean against the couch. When she heard Sandy walk out of the room, she closed her eyes again.

"Always goes better? You do this often?"

She sat there for a second before turning to answer Brent's question. He sounded genuinely curious. Turning slowly, she curled up in the corner of the couch and looked over at him. He gave her an uncertain smile. "I try not to do this at all, actually." She shrugged. "But a few times I've passed out, when I've been unprepared or didn't know what I was getting into." She looked down into her cup. "And yeah, soon I'm going to bottom out and sleep like a rock for hours."

Brent leaned forward, the necklace still dangling from one hand. "I'll get to some sort of logical questions at some point, but for now, I mean—wow!"

Jac grinned at his words, she felt like she wanted to cry. This was the first time in her life anyone had taken it this calmly. She sniffled. "It's really not so *wow* on my end of things." Looking over at Reid, his back to her still, she sighed. He still hadn't looked at her. Taking a shaky breath, she looked back at Brent. He had followed where she was looking and offered her a helpless shrug. She cleared her throat. "There's beer and stuff in the kitchen if you'd like something."

Brent smirked at her and understood. "I'll go see if anything appeals, thanks." He stood up and looked over at his partner's ridged stance. "Want anything, Reid?" The other man just shook his head.

Jac sat there watching him. His back was straight and tense. "Reid?" He didn't turn or speak, just held up his hand asking her for a moment more. Her whole body felt heavier now. Turning, she drooped sideways, her head supported by the back of the couch, so she didn't have to expend any further energy to stay upright. She could hear the other two talking quietly in the kitchen.

Reid turned slowly, still looking down at the angel he held in his hand. Finally looking up from his hand, he looked at her for a few silent minutes. She was curled into the corner of the couch, trying to hide in it. He looked like he had so many thoughts going through his head at once, he couldn't grasp onto one. He looked down at his hand again. "I don't believe in this."

"In angels or what I just did?" She asked softly.

His eyes moved to her. "Both."

She thought for a moment. "Neither do I." She gave him a serious look. "In angels that is, as hard as I try to not believe I can do this, I've never been able to escape it."

"You mean run?"

She shrugged. "A bit of both."

He took a few steps toward her then stopped. "Since the moment I met you, things haven't added up. But I couldn't or wouldn't have drawn this conclusion." He clenched his jaw a few times. "Why did you change your name, Jacinda?" His voice was shaking.

"For all the reasons I told you before, I just didn't tell you how I helped."

Reid moved quietly over to the chair and leaned against it and continued to study her. "People found out." She nodded. "How many times have you had to relocate?"

She sighed and focused on her empty cup. "Three. This is the longest time…" She didn't know what to say, so she just sat there waiting for his logic to kick in.

He put the angel pendant into his pocket and sat down, placing his hands in his lap. "Your phobia of being near strangers, this explains it."

Jac nodded. "I learned at a young age that even accidentally touching the wrong person can bring me to my knees if they're angry or filled with other strong or violent emotions."

Reid let out a long breath. He leaned back and watched her for a moment. She was fighting to stay conscious now, her eyes growing heavier. Turning his head, he looked towards the kitchen. "You two can stop hiding in there now."

Jac chuckled quietly to herself. She could picture them peeking around the corner waiting for the battle to begin. Brent came around the corner first, he was smirking.

"How dangerous was what you did today?" Reid asked quietly.

She turned back to see the serious green eyes studying her again. "It was …"

"Really stupid." Sandy finished for her as she walked into the room carrying a plate of cheese and crackers.

Jac sighed and took the plate. "I had to try, Sandy."

Reid leaned forward in the chair, taking the can he was handed. "Try what? Exactly"

Brent nodded. "Yeah, cuz from where we were sitting you looked like you were just sitting there looking around."

She took a few nibbles of cheese before looking at him. "I didn't get anything from the first few. Mostly because they were found on surfaces that don't hold vibrations." She took the cup Sandy held out to her. "Wood and metal seem to hold the strongest images for the longest time."

"The factory and boat," Reid stated quietly.

Jac nodded; handing the plate back to Sandy she shook her head. It was past the point where she had the energy to eat. Lifting her head, she looked over at Brent for a moment, then to Reid. "I saw him." She said quietly. "Through their eyes." A tear rolled down her face. "Elaine was so strong, right until that last moment, she never faltered." She glanced at Sandy, who had her hand over her mouth and terror in her eyes. "And I can never let her father and sister know." Taking a deep breath, she tried to calm herself. "Later, I'll see if I can sit for a sketch or something." She looked at Brent for a moment, not sure of the expression in his eyes. "Just please, run those blood tests again from Ms. Thomas, she was so groggy and incoherent, maybe we can trace a substance or something." Reid nodded, leaning forward, a look of pain and mixed emotions in his eyes. "The clothes part has been driving me nuts." She took an unsteady sip of the tea. She had to hurry, she felt like she was being pulled down into a dark hole. "They struggled and fought, yet their clothes were perfect. There was no sign of a break-in at their homes…"

Brent nodded again. "I'll see if any of the relatives were aware of a trip."

Nodding, she rested her head back against the couch again. Taking a deep breath, she grinned and tried to keep her eyes open. "I'm done."

Sandy wiped the tears off her own cheeks and got up. "Come on, we'll get you to bed, and then I'll camp out here with a good book or something." She was just reaching down when her pager went off. She straightened up and pulled it off her belt. "Damn." Looking at it she grimaced. "I'm on suicide watch this week, I'll be right back." She walked quickly over to her purse.

Jac chuckled and looked at the confused look on Brent's face. "Oh yeah, did I ever tell you what kind of Doctor Sandy is?"

She opened her eyes wider when Reid's voice was much closer. "I'm going to say head doctor." He didn't give her a chance to object, just reached down and scooped her up into his arms, holding her against his chest. "Point the way."

She was more shocked that he was helping her, than she was by anything that had taken place all day. Lifting her arm, she pointed towards the short hallway. She was glad she was too exhausted and out of it to pick up any emotions right now, so she took the opportunity to rest her head against his shoulder. Grasping at the rare moment she could feel like everyone else, she cuddled a little closer to him.

"I thought you couldn't touch me?"

His breath was on her cheek. She smirked against his neck. "I'm too pooped to pick up on anything right now." She sighed. "It's wonderful, the only time in my life I get to feel normal, like everyone else does."

Reid grinned at the sleepy tone of her voice. Walking into the bedroom, he went quickly over to her bed, lowering her onto it. Leaning down, with a hand on either side of her, he looked at the heavy brown eyes as they opened again. "Later, when you're all there again, we'll talk." She nodded, continuing to look at him.

She didn't hesitate for the first time he could recall and placed a hand gently against his cheek. "Thanks for not sending me to the funny farm," she whispered.

He grinned. "I'm still trying to decide if I should go there for a vacation." He put his hand over hers still against his skin. Pulling it into his own he turned his head and kissed her palm. "Get some rest."

She closed her eyes, sighing; her fingers curled around his kiss then rested her fist against her chest, letting the sleep take her.

Reid stood there, watching her for a moment, before letting out a deep breath. He walked to the end of the bed, pulling a blanket over her. Rubbing his jaw, he looked at her again. In his world, his job, there were concrete things—laws of what was and what wasn't that couldn't be broken, no matter what. It was a constant in his world. Was. Now he didn't know what to trust as fact. The woman lying there had just blown it all away. There was so much to process, once he had the chance.

14

Reid walked back to the living room and found the doctor pulling on her jacket.

"I'm sorry, I planned to stay and talk after she fell asleep." Sandy looked towards the bedroom. "If I hurry, I can get back before the nightmares start."

Reid's eyebrows went up. "Nightmares?"

Sandy nodded picking up her purse. "I imagine she'll relive those women's last moments this time." She shook her head with disgust. "It's just one of the many prices she has to pay for an ability she doesn't want."

Reid ran his hand through his hair. "I can stay until you get back."

She stopped as she reached for the door and gave him a hesitant look. "Oh, that would be wonderful, then I don't have to try to rush through an emotional crisis with another patient." She walked over to the table and picked up a notepad.

Brent held up his hand, and then looked at Reid. "I'm going to get back to the station, I want to start checking Jac's theories."

Reid put his head down. He must be tired; he'd forgotten about the case completely. He looked at Brent and nodded. "Call me if anything turns up."

Brent nodded, and then turned back to the woman hovering by the door. "Can I catch a lift with you?"

Sandy smiled and nodded. Pausing she studied Reid. "I've

written down my numbers, they're by the phone, the tea she drinks is on the counter." She paused for a second. "If she does wake up long enough, see if you can get her to eat or just drink some juice."

Reid stuffed his hands in his pockets. "Will do."

She looked at him a moment longer, smiled, then she and Brent went through the door.

Reid turned and looked around the room. He wasn't quite sure what he was doing here, if he was honest with himself, he just felt he needed to stay. Sighing, he stuck his head in the kitchen and spotted the tea canister and cup on the counter. Straightening, he looked down the hallway. She'll relive those women's last moments this time… It kept running through his mind. He would bet money that Jac knew it would happen but had moved forward, to help them. Turning, he went into the kitchen and grabbed a bottle of juice out of the fridge.

He walked into her room, he went and sat down in the chair facing her bed. She was still sleeping exactly as he'd left her.

~

Reid sat watching her as small pieces from the last week started to fit together slowly. Little cues she had given away. Not once has she lied, just hadn't filled in all the blanks.

The ability to look at something and not see the same thing everyone else does. She had said that when they first met in her office, it meant an entirely different thing to him now.

When she moved, he sat perfectly still, barely breathing, not wanting to disturb her.

He didn't believe in things like this. He'd heard all the stories, read about it often. Yet he couldn't help but believe her. Some things you couldn't fake, this was one of those. Knowing and actually believing made more sense now. She made more sense now. The little things she did that aroused his suspicions. He smirked. You were right detective, she was hiding something, and it was a hell of a something. He sighed and looked back at her, if his hormones weren't constantly getting in the way, he may have figured a few more things out.

When the nightmares started, he watched her struggle against things he couldn't see. He tried touching her, to bring her out of it and that only seemed to make it worse. She cried out anytime he got too close. Was what he was feeling affecting her in some way?

When she calmed, he hurried to make the tea. Probably more to feel like he was actually doing something.

When they started again, watching her relive the moments was breaking his heart. No, that was not even close, it felt more like someone was pulling it out through his throat. Just watching her convulse and contorted in what looked like pain was more than he could take. She was incoherent and mumbling anytime he'd thought she was waking.

When she'd cried out 'help me' during one of the turbulent moments of unrest, he had been ready to drop to his knees beside the bed and beg her to let him know how he could do anything that would end this.

Reid sat beside the bed, he sat in the corner and kept moving the damn chair all over the room. When he couldn't find a new place to put the chair, he stood and watched her. Sighing, he put the chair beside the dresser and sat down, leaning his arm against the dresser and watched her. How long before she would wake up? Why hadn't he thought of these questions when the doctor was still here?

~

Jacinda woke up feeling sore and hungry. She frowned. It wasn't the first time. She turned her head to see Reid slumped in a chair beside her dresser. Sitting up slowly she looked around. There were two cups and a half bottle of apple juice on the table beside her. He had stayed. Why? Where was Sandy?

"You're awake."

She looked to see him pulling himself up in the chair. "Yeah." She regarded the cups again. "Thanks for looking after me." She brushed her hair away from her face. "Was it bad?"

Reid sat forward and grimaced as if his whole body objected to the movement. "Well, as this was my first watch, I'm not sure." He stood up and stretched. "But you scared the breath right out of me a few times." Walking over, he squatted down beside the bed as his eyes roamed over her face. "Do you remember it when you wake up?"

Jac shook her head. "Rarely." She smirked. "A few times, I've asked Sandy why she's here, I thought she was going to hit me."

He grinned. "From the awake person's perspective, I'd understand if she did. It's not like any kind of nightmare I've ever experienced, you were physically struggling and…" He shook his head. "I decided about three hours in, when we get this guy, I'm shooting him." Her hand flew up to her mouth. He sighed. "I won't, would like to, but won't."

She frowned at him for a moment. "Where is Sandy?"

"Suicide watch, or call, or something."

"Ah." Jac blew out a breath. "I need to get up and move around, I'm so sore."

"Do you need a hand?"

She thought for a second. "Just don't go too far. My body is running on nothing right now."

Reid stood up and held out his hand to her. She sat there looking at it. Sighing he bent down and pulled the sleeve of her sweatshirt down over her hand, then straightened holding out his hand again. "You must love winter when it's cold enough for gloves."

She smiled. "Love it." Reaching up she placed her sleeve-covered hand in his as he pulled her to the edge of the bed. Standing slowly, she gripped his hand tightly. "Legs are really wobbly."

Reaching he carefully placed his other hand on her covered waist. "Let's aim for the couch okay?" She nodded as she took a few shaky steps.

Finally reaching the couch she dropped down onto it. "Have you heard anything from Brent?"

Reid shook his head. "I called a few times last night; he was half asleep on his desk, waiting for the toxicology reports."

She chewed her lip. "Let him sleep a bit then."

Reid stood there looking at her. She was still pale. "You should try eating something."

Jac sighed. "There's oatmeal in the cupboard, it always goes down best." She chewed her lip again. "I want to see if we can get a sketch of the man I saw."

He nodded. "We can do that after you eat—I'll be right back."

~

Reid and Jac sat studying the picture sitting on the table. Jac hesitantly looked over at him, quietly she spoke, "Thank you for getting someone that doesn't know I'm unofficially helping on this."

He shrugged. "I didn't think you were up to going down to the station yet and Rick owes me a few favors." He looked at the picture again, studying it. "It's too bad he had a hat on."

Jac frowned at the drawing. "It was never quite clear enough to show me what color his hair was that the hat didn't cover."

He rubbed his hand over his face. "It's clearer than the video, we can see his face."

She smirked. "I guess my wiring is better." Stretching she looked at the picture again. "So, the best next step is to check the male profiles with this?" She yawned.

He glanced at the clock. "It's the only option we have right now unless some new lead falls from the sky." Leaning on the table he searched her face. "Listen it's barely even ten yet, why don't you grab a nap, while I run home and grab a shower, then we'll get some work done."

"On a normal day I'd argue, but not today." Jac stood up. He watched her carefully. "Relax; my legs aren't rubber anymore." Her cell phone rang. Reid handed it to her before she had a chance to locate it. "Hello."

"Jac. How are you doing?"

Jac rolled her eyes at Reid. "I'm okay, Sandy."

"I'm just getting out of the hospital now. I have appointments, I'm so sorry I had to leave last night."

Jac grinned. "It's okay, you have a job. You're not my babysitter." She smirked when Reid pointed to himself. "Reid stayed and looked after me."

"Really? And how's that going?"

She could hear the wheels turning inside the doctor's head. "Everything's fine."

"Not the details I was asking for. Listen, I have to run. You stay home today and keep your feet up, doctors' orders."

Jac laughed. "You're a head doctor, Sandy." She could hear the traffic in the background.

"Doesn't matter I'm still a doctor. I'm not kidding, you don't know what could happen after that stunt yesterday…"

Jac held up a hand. "Fine, I'll take it easy. Now get off the phone crazy lady before you drive over someone."

Sandy laughed. "Yes mother. I'll call you later."

"Okay, talk to you soon." She hung up the phone and looked at Reid. "I've been told to stay at home and relax today." She rolled her eyes at him. "Sandy is worried."

He frowned. "Okay, so we'll look at profiles from here." He shrugged. "There's not much I can do at the office right now, it all comes down to finding him." He pointed to the sketch again. Pulling out his wallet he held out a card to her. "Call if you need me before I get back." She took it and nodded.

15

Jac still felt out of it, she had no energy, even after the nap. Sandy was right, although she'd never tell her, she'd never done anything like what she'd done yesterday, and she would never do it again. Usually, it took her a few hours and a nap to feel fully charged again.

By the time Reid returned she'd had a nap and a shower. That made her feel a bit more alert, at least.

Reid studied her for a few minutes, his eyes filled with concern. "Are you sure you're okay?"

She shrugged. "I guess yesterday took a lot more out of me than I thought." She smirked. "I've never purposely tried to see that much all at once."

He sat down at the table and looked over his laptop at her. "You could have told us what you were doing…" She raised an eyebrow at him. "Okay, maybe not, but did you have to do it all at once?"

Jac studied him for a moment. She wasn't prepared for questions about her sight. "I think I did, yes. Each time the vision was clearer." Leaning on her elbows, she rubbed her temples. "It was like a paint-by-numbers in a way, each time the features were more visible, although it could have something to do with the difference in time that had passed too."

"I don't understand—a lot, but until you look like you're yourself again I'm going to stay curious."

She smirked at him. "I really feel completely drained, still, and I don't like it."

Reid got up and picked up the laptop. "Let's take this into the couch, where you can flake and browse through profiles."

She was touched by his concern and consideration. This was the man she was sure had no emotions or at least none that he ever let show. The last day had shown her a different man. The way he was at the funeral, trying to shield and protect her.

"This would work better if you came to the couch."

Jac looked up to see him leaning against the doorframe smirking at her. "Sorry, my mind wandered."

He laughed. "That's okay, if my mind had gone through what yours did it would probably take a long vacation." His phone rang. Motioning for her to go to the couch he answered it.

Wiggling around on the couch until she found a comfortable position, she huffed out a breath. Even that tired her. Pulling the table a bit closer, she brought up the search page. Glancing down at the sketch again she studied it. *How old are you? Where do I start?* Other than male, she wasn't entirely sure what to put in the search. He looked over thirty. Decision made, she typed in thirty to forty-five and hit enter.

The enthusiasm, she was already lacking flagged even more when she saw more than two hundred hits. This is going to take forever. Quickly she selected Caucasian and it dropped down to one seventy. Better. This would take all day.

Reid watched her for a few minutes. "Brent is going to come over with the toxicology report."

She looked up. "Oh good."

~

Brent walked quietly into the room after Reid warned him to be quiet. He glanced back over his shoulder at Reid. "Is it normal for her to sleep this much after?"

Reid shrugged. "I don't know." He motioned him into the kitchen. "She said she's never done that much all at once before."

"Have you called a doctor?"

Reid gave him an annoyed look. "And say what? My friend is really lethargic after reading the visions from a dead woman left in the woods?"

Brent scowled. "Good point." He glanced in at the woman sleeping on the couch again. "Has she been drinking that tea? Have you called Doctor Gains? She's the only one that knows what she goes through."

Reid rubbed his jaw. "Jacinda said if I try to make her drink any more she's going to scream, and I'm pretty sure she meant it. My guess is Doctor Gains will be showing up as soon as she can get away."

Brent nodded. "So, do we wake her and tell her she was right?" He pulled the papers from his pocket.

Reid glanced at her, contemplating. "I have a feeling she'd be really unhappy if we didn't."

Brent elbowed him. "Still afraid of her temper?"

Reid rolled his eyes and walked back over to the couch. She looked so pale and was missing something, what had Brent called it? Vibrancy? She looked so at peace; he really second-guessed himself before he bent down and lightly touched her shoulder. "Jacinda." Her eyes slowly opened. "Brent's here with the report."

She smiled at him. "Sorry, I didn't mean to fade on you." She turned her head and looked at Brent standing at the end of the couch. "Hey."

Brent smiled. "Hey, sleeping beauty." He perched on the end of the couch. "This guy been looking after you?"

She sat up a little bit. "Very well actually."

Brent nodded. "Good. Are you up to some shop talk?"

She made a small gesture with her head. "Maybe it will keep me awake." She glanced at the screen.

Brent held up the paper. "You were right; there were traces of alcohol and a drug, commonly used for date rape in Ms. Thomas's blood." Jac turned her head and looked at him for a moment. When she started to chew on her lip, the men looked at each other.

She regarded Reid for a moment, and then looked down to the sketch on the table. "I think she knew him." Their eyebrows went up. "I don't mean through the dating site, outside of it."

Reid slid down to sit across from her. "Why do you say that?"

She sat up a bit more. "The others weren't groggy or incoherent, they were completely alert." She closed her eyes for a moment. "Her feelings were different, too. There was no panic, not like with the others…" She trailed off, closing her eyes again. Opening them she looked at Reid. "She had so much animosity, the other's emotions were much different. This sort of anger and hatred you could really only have towards someone you knew. If it were a stranger, wouldn't fear be more prominent?"

Reid looked at her for a moment and then to Brent. "I think she's got something, again."

Brent nodded slowly. "Yeah." He looked over at Jac and smiled. "We may have to keep you when all of this is done."

Jac laughed. "I would love to help with the research part, really, but I think I'm done dealing with murder, thank you."

Reid leaned forward, giving her a serious look. "After what you went through, I'm saying you are never doing that to yourself again."

Brent gave him a shocked look, then Jac a concerned one.

Jac nodded. "He doesn't want to have to shoot too many people."

Brent looked at his partner again. "Shoot…"

"I said I wanted to, not that I would."

Brent let out a breath. "I don't want to know." He sat down and looked at the sketch sitting on the table. "This who we want?"

Reid nodded. "Most definitely." He motioned towards the laptop. "We're checking the male profiles to see if he's in it there." He knew Brent would think the same thing; the chances of finding him that way were slim.

Brent glanced from the sketch back to him. "Can he have an unpublished profile and still contact women?"

Reid looked at Jac.

She shook her head. "No, you can look but not make contact."

Brent sat back. "So, where do we go from here?"

Reid rubbed his jaw again. "We have to hope he's got a visible profile."

Brent blew out a breath. "Okay then, let me get a copy of this sketch. I can look and hold down the fort at the office."

Reid sat up again. "Sounds good, you go get a copy while we have something to eat."

Jac just looked at him. She chewed her lip for a minute, causing both men to stop and watch her again. "You guys have to stop doing that." Brent winked at her. "Is there…" She looked down at the sketch again. "Can we find out if Ms. Thomas had, I'm not sure, a bad investment that resulted in a large money loss." She sighed. "I'm not sure what I'm thinking, but I just know there has to be a connection there."

Brent rubbed his jaw in thought. "She must have had an accountant. I can check it out."

Reid nodded. "Do that and we'll continue the profiles." He grinned at Jac. "Now, I'll get you something to eat."

Jac grimaced. "No more tea."

He laughed as he walked towards the kitchen.

Jac threw up her hands. "I can't look at another one."

Reid nodded from his slumped position on the couch. "Neither can I."

She sat forward in the chair, pushing the laptop to the center of the table. "I can't believe we went through that whole group." She rubbed her face. "How is Brent doing?"

Reid smirked. "He was going to finish up the twenty-five to thirty age groups and go home. His only comment was that there really are a lot of slimy guys out there."

She giggled. "Well, if you were a woman, you'd already know this."

His eyebrows went up. "You sound like you speak from experience."

She nodded. "Oh yes. The joys of love and infidelity."

He looked at her for a moment. "Been there done that." Her jaw dropped. He held up his hands. "I was the victim."

Her cheeks flushed with embarrassment. "Sorry." The phone rang, making her lose what she was going to say next. Stretching over, she picked it up. "Hello."

"Hi, sorry I didn't get there. The last twenty-four hours have been straight out of an action movie."

She grinned. "That's okay, doctor, everything is fine here."

"That sexy detective still hanging around?"

"Yes. We've been working on the case."

"What happened to relaxing?"

Jac frowned. "I've been napping off and on all day."

"I wondered how this would affect you. Let me know how you are in the morning, and if you're not back to normal we should think about a doctor."

Jac grinned at the concern in her voice. "Yeah, that will happen." She smirked.

"I know I know. Okay, I have to go lie down or I'm going to fall down."

Jac nodded. "I understand, get some rest." She hung up the phone and smirked over at Reid. "Sandy is just getting to bed now from yesterday."

He raised his eyebrows. "And I thought my job was tops at depriving me of that much sleep."

She shrugged. "She's just dedicated to her patients." Scowling at the laptop, she sighed. "I think I've had enough research for one day."

He nodded. "Yeah, when leads dry up it gets a little tiresome. I'm sure you've run into that before though."

"Most of the time, the research I'm doing it easy to trace, it occasionally gets tedious." She stretched. "Now I'm stiff from just sitting around all day." He just sat there watching her in an odd way. She tilted her head and looked at him. "What?"

He blinked and then raised his hands. "Last night I thought of so many questions and now when I'd like to ask one, I can't even remember any." He studied his hands he'd clasped together. "I really don't buy into stuff like this, normally."

She chuckled. "That's good. Having your feet planted firmly on the ground would be good in your line of work, I'm sure you see a lot of real nut cases."

He grimaced. "Oh, yeah. If I hadn't been with you yesterday, you would have fit into that nut case category too for a bit."

She smiled. "That's okay, really. It wouldn't be the first time."

He sat back and blew out a long breath while studying her. "No, I guess not." She sat there watching him. "It's been a hard road, hasn't it?"

She cast her eyes down at the floor for a few seconds, then back at him. "Yes, it has. I've had to give up everything and everyone more than once, and I can't tell you how happy I am that you and Brent didn't try to take me to the mental hospital last night."

He realized at that moment, that no matter what he'd been through in his life, it would never compare to the heartache she'd suffered. Suffered all because she wasn't what the rest of the world considered normal. "Do you have family anywhere?"

She shook her head. "There was only my parents and I lost them to a boating accident almost ten years ago now."

"No other relatives?"

"Not that I know of." Her voice was clipped, letting him know she didn't want to discuss it.

"I'm all that's left too." It startled him that he'd told her, he never really told anyone that, in that way.

She frowned. "It sucks, doesn't it?"

He shrugged. "At times. All the guys complain about family things they have to go to and sometimes I think they don't know what they're talking about."

"No, they don't. Until I met Sandy, I really had no one."

Reid nodded. Reaching over he closed the laptop. "Feel like going for a walk? If I don't breathe in some fresh air soon, I'm going to go crazy."

She thought about it for a moment. "I'd like that."

16

They'd walked around her whole neighborhood. Hardly speaking. For a moment, she'd wished she could hold his hand. That was the first time in her life she'd ever wanted to hold someone's hand.

"It's quiet here."

She looked up at him. "Yeah, I love it here." She glanced through the fence at the quiet grassy park. "I don't do well in apartment buildings filled with people, this place may cost me more, but the peace makes it all worth it."

"You make enough with your work?"

She grinned. "Sometimes, not so much other times." She put her hands in her pockets, keeping her eyes on the faded sidewalk. "I've actually been thinking about trying to find a different office."

"You don't like your closet office?"

She smirked at him. "No, not particularly."

"Such a shame…" It surprised him when she reached over, giving him a playful shove. He stopped and leered down at her. "That is not fair at all and you know it. I'm completely afraid to touch you, in case I make you, I don't know what exactly."

She laughed at him. "A casual touch from someone I know, as long as they're not mad doesn't hurt or cause anything."

He stood there studying her. "Really?" She nodded. "And when I kissed you in the closet, okay that does sound funny. It didn't bother you?"

She smirked at him again. "I don't think so, it was so brief I really couldn't tell."

He grinned down at her. Her brown eyes seemed to be taunting him. He stood there in front of her for a moment then smiled. Slowly he reached out to gently cup the back of her head. Her eyes didn't leave his, as he lowered his mouth to slowly brush against hers. He lifted his head and looked down at her for a moment. He didn't want to scare her or harm her in any way, but he had to have a taste.

When his mouth touched hers again, he felt her hands move up to his chest. Her mouth was warm and welcoming. He wanted to crush her against him but didn't know what he could and couldn't do as far as she was concerned. He lifted his head, resting his forehead against hers. Those brown eyes looking at him were hazy. "I'm not going to cause you to have a seizure or something, am I?"

She stood there looking at him and then smiled. "Just don't think of the last person you shot or anything like that and we're good."

He grinned and lifted his head to look down at her. "You make it sound like I go around shooting people." He was enjoying the feel of her hands against his chest more than he thought he would.

"Don't you?" She smiled at him in a teasing way.

He reached, putting a hand behind her waist and pulled her closer. "No." Running his hand down the back of her silky hair he smirked. "You can be sure when I'm kissing you, that you will be the only thing I am thinking about." Her smile was inviting, her eyes told him…

"Does this mean we're done working for the day?"

They turned to find Brent standing and leaning on the roof of his car, stopped in the middle of the street. Grinning at them like the proverbial cat that caught the canary.

Reid cleared his throat. "We are."

Brent frowned. "You could have let me know. I tried calling and when I got no answer, I lit out of the office so fast I'm not sure if I closed a single door behind me."

Reid released her but kept a hand loosely around her waist. "We needed to get out of there for a bit."

"Uh huh." Brent winked at Jac. "At least he's not dragging

you in closets now."

Jac looked down at the ground, blushing. "No, he's not."

Reid smirked. "The reason you were calling was?"

Brent straightened. "To tell you I've had it and I'm going home to sleep."

Reid nodded. "Okay. See you at the office in the morning."

Brent nodded then grinned at Jac. "Are you coming in tomorrow?"

She nodded. "Absolutely. Tomorrow is the day we find him."

"I hope so." He nodded once abruptly, then got back in his car and drove away without another word.

"I should get going too." Reid looked down at her. Still a little speechless that she blushed.

She smiled. "Yeah, believe it or not I'm starting to feel kind of tired."

He stood back and studied her. "Are you all right?"

She leaned closer to him. "Yeah, I think by tomorrow I'll be up and running again."

He put his arm around her casually, walking back the few houses to her place.

Neither spoke when he came in with her to get his phone and keys.

He stood at the door for a moment. She stood looking up at him, saying nothing that helped him know what she was thinking. Stepping closer, he grinned down at her. "This is breaking my number one rule, with us working together, but ..." He lowered his head and gently brushed his mouth over hers. Her hand moved to rest on his chest again. He lifted his head and smirked. "I've never been good with rules." He cupped the back of her head in his hand and pulled her, so her mouth was against his again. With his other hand he pulled her hips so her whole body was nestled against his. And dammit it, she felt so *right* against him.

His tongue tasted every dark corner in her mouth, when her hands went up into his hair, he was ready to pick her up and push his own restraint to the limit.

Resting his forehead against hers, he stood there with his eyes closed for a moment, willing his breathing to calm down. "Are you all right?"

"Mmm, more than." She whispered against his mouth.

He almost groaned as the raspy words brushed against his lips. "I'll pick you up in the morning, we're going to get this guy, then, we're going to see where this goes." He lifted his head and looked down at her. Just seeing her eyes half closed looking up at him made him want to throw away all the rules and stay right here.

She smiled up at him. "Okay."

He took a deep breath, starting to let go of her, then pulled her against him again and kissed her hard, not giving her time to object. Her mouth responded to his with abandon, making him wonder what the rest would be like. Pulling his mouth away he held her, his face in her hair, breathing in her scent. He began kissing the soft skin on her neck, gently. Groaning he lifted his head. "I have to go." He squeezed her against him briefly, and then backed up. "Get some rest. I'll see you in the morning."

She couldn't find any words, so she just nodded and smiled at him.

He backed towards the door, turning before he hit it and left quickly. Standing outside for a moment, he shook his head and went to his car. As if he didn't already have enough motivation to find this killer, with a smirk as he climbed in and quickly headed home.

Jac stood there looking at the closed door. She'd never felt that way when someone was kissing her. Her head was spinning, her knees actually were weak. She hadn't wanted him to stop. His strong arm around her made her feel completely protected, his mouth teased in a way she didn't think she'd ever felt. She ran a shaking hand over her mouth and smiled. Didn't see that coming did you mystic one? She grinned to herself, walked around turning the lights off. She was sure there would be no bad dreams tonight.

~

She was wrong. Twice she woke up to find herself panting and soaked in sweat. The nightmares didn't usually continue after the first day. She lay there staring at the clock, afraid to go back to sleep. Sandy would have a fit if she called her at this time of night. Of course, she'd insist on coming straight over, but Jac didn't want to do that to her. She'd already done a twenty-seven-hour day or more, as her sense of time was all out of whack from sleeping so much.

Jac turned her head and looked at the card she'd set on the table when she'd had her nap. What would he think if she woke him at this time of night? His concern was genuine, she knew. She could feel when he kissed her; his fear of causing something to happen was right up front. Of course, she hadn't felt it long, or hadn't been focused long enough to feel it, she wasn't sure which. Sighing she picked up the card. Always better to find these things out in the beginning, she thought, as she reached for the phone. She felt guilty when his sleepy voice came out of the phone.

"Hey, sorry to wake you."

"Jacinda? What's wrong?"

The concern in his voice made her feel better. "Nightmares."

She heard him move, probably sitting up. "Do you want me to come over? Are they as bad as last night?"

She shook her head. "No, I'm able to get out of them, just afraid to sleep now. You don't have to come over; I just needed someone to talk to." She sighed. "Sorry I woke you…"

"Don't be." He sighed. "It's fine."

"But you sound so sleepy."

He laughed. "I sound sleepy until I've had at least a full pot of coffee, which is why I don't talk in the mornings."

Just hearing him was soothing. "I would have called Sandy, but she tends to yell when she's awakened, and I'm pretty sure that wouldn't help."

"It's okay, I don't mind really. I'd much rather talk to you…" He paused. "At two in the morning, then Brent, he mumbles."

She laughed. "I never really thanked you for everything…"

"Hey, it's fine. If I was half the cop everyone keeps telling me I am, I'd have caught this guy a while ago and you never would have had to do what you did."

She pouted at the phone. "But then we wouldn't have met."

"Good point. Okay I'm glad I'm a poor cop." She laughed again. "We're going to get him, Jacinda, very soon, you've been a monumental help with every good lead we've got."

"More flukes really." She played with the trim on her comforter.

He laughed. "I don't think so, but my ego appreciates your saying so." She yawned. "You really need to get some rest, or I'll take you to see a doctor."

She sighed. "That would be mean. I don't like being a guinea pig."

He was silent for a few seconds. "Nah, I'd tell them you had a big scare or something."

She smirked. "I didn't think officers lied…"

He laughed deeply. "Oh, right, we're perfect all the time."

"I guess I should let you get some sleep, so you don't growl at people tomorrow."

He groaned. "I don't growl."

"Oh yes you do." She smiled to herself in the dark. "I do feel better, Reid. Thank you."

"Call if you need me again." His voice was a soft whisper.

"I hope not, but okay. See you when the sun shines."

"Yep." She waited. "Good night, Jacinda."

She closed her eyes and smiled. "Good night, Reid." Hanging up the phone, she kept her eyes closed so she could keep his voice inside her head. Maybe that would be enough to keep the nightmares at bay.

17

Jac climbed in the car the next morning with a smile on her face. "Good morning."

He smiled and handed her a cup of coffee. "Sleep better after I threatened you with a doctor?"

She laughed. "That was a threat? I did manage to sleep." She sniffed the coffee. "Thank you."

"You're welcome." He leaned over and lightly grasped the back of her head and pulled her towards him. He kissed her softly on the lips and started to lift his head. Inhaling deeply, he kissed her again, roughly before resting his forehead against hers. "You are ruining my impeccable work ethics."

Jac smiled. "Um, sorry?"

He straightened away from her and shook his head as he put the car into drive.

The good feelings ended when they walked into the office and saw the Captain there with Brent, studying the sketch.

Brent looked over and smiled at Jac. "Good morning."

She grinned. "Morning." She nodded to the Captain. "Hello."

The Captain studied her. "Feeling better today? Detective Jordan told me you had a touch of the flu yesterday."

She gave Brent a quick look and then smiled. "I'm much better today, all I wanted to do yesterday was sleep."

The Captain nodded, and then held up the sketch. "I hear we have you to thank for this, finding out there was a video. Too bad we couldn't print a copy from the video, but a sketch works fine, great work, Miss Brown."

She just stood there looking back at him. "Thank you."

The Captain nudged Brent. "Everyone upstairs is buzzing around now that we have a face to look for." He grinned. "We may have to bring her in on other cases that have thrown so many variables at us."

Reid leaned against his desk and nodded. "She'd be great at the computer while we run around."

Jac didn't miss him basically saying she wasn't doing any seeing for police work in the future. "Anytime you're out of ideas." She smirked at Reid.

The Captain turned to Reid, and then looked at Brent. "I want you two to find out who runs that dating site and have a discussion with them, they need to know what activities are being connected to their business."

Brent nodded. "We'll get something set up."

The Captain nodded once. "Keep me posted."

He handed her the sketch as he walked out. She stood there waiting until she was sure he couldn't hear then turned to them. "I feel awful. You guys are lying for me?"

Reid laughed. "Don't, we only tell the Captain what we think he really needs to hear."

Brent grinned. "It's more peaceful that way."

She studied them for a moment. "Oh. Well, don't stretch things too far." She held up the sketch. "If he ever wants to see that video, he'll know there is no way this could come from it."

Reid shrugged. "He won't."

"What about the others, didn't they ask questions?"

Brent shook his head. "Sketch artist took off the glasses. And no, everyone else is just happy to have something to work with."

She chewed her lip and looked back down at the sketch, the sketch of the man that had been strangling her in her dreams the past two nights. She looked up when a hand pulled it from her.

Reid shook his head. "I think you've seen enough of this guy for now." He smiled at her. "Think you can get to Mrs. Oster one more time and get us some sort of meeting?"

She nodded. "Just as soon as I've finished my coffee."

Brent watched the exchange. They stood closer and were just standing there looking at each other now. He wasn't certain if this was better than them biting at each other. "While you're doing that, Reid and I are going to look into your packed bag idea."

Reid looked over at him. "You didn't get that done yesterday?"

Brent laughed. "My face was only a few inches off that keyboard all day yesterday. Longest day of my life."

Reid laughed. "We'll try to keep this one shorter for you."

"That would be great." He walked over to his desk feeling better about getting back into work mode.

After fifteen minutes of persuading and chatting, Jac finally managed to get the owners names from Mrs. Oster and a meeting set up. She hung up the phone and turned around to wait for both men to be off the phones. "Alan Howard, Edward Lawson and you have a meeting with them at three."

Brent frowned. "I'm going over to the victims…" He gave her an apologetic look. "To Desi Sloan's place at three, her housemate said a bag wasn't there, one that she had set out the day before her death."

Reid shrugged. "No big deal, Jacinda can come with me, maybe she can help me convince these two there's a problem."

"I can try." She got up and wrote the two names on the board beside Love Quest. She looked over at Reid. "Do we need to look up anything on them?"

He shrugged. "I'm going to check for prior convictions, so I know who I'm dealing with."

Brent stood up. "I'm going to go get coffee and something that looks like food. Anyone need anything?"

Jac wandered back over to her chair. "Tea and a danish please."

Reid shrugged. "Just coffee thanks." He watched his partner walk out of the room. He looked over at her sitting at her desk. She was still going through profiles. Getting up, he walked over and closed the door, and then moved over to her and put his hands on the back of the chair. "Haven't you looked at everyone yet?"

She frowned up at him. "Sadly, no." He turned her chair slowly, so she was facing him. Those sexy as hell brown eyes searched his face and when her expression changed, he knew that she realized what he was doing. She glanced quickly towards the door. "Reid, we're in your office."

He nodded. "Yeah, we are." He scowled. "I don't have a closet here."

She grinned at him. "Anyone could walk in." He nodded again, not taking his eyes from her mouth. "Brent…"

"Will stop and talk to every person he sees along the way, he *loves* people."

She smirked at him. He was leaning down on the arms of her chair, his eyes moving all over her face. When his hand gently stroked down her cheek, she smiled at him. "Reid…" Her own voice was a whisper.

He slowly lowered his head and brushed his mouth against hers. Lingering for a few seconds longer he straightened up. He sighed. "I should arrest you for interfering with police investigations." He moved his hand to the back of her head and kissed her roughly.

"I was behaving." She whispered breathlessly as he released her.

He ran his hand down her cheek again. "I know and it was distracting the hell out of me."

She laughed. "Then you better arrest yourself first."

He touched his thumb against her bottom lip before he stood up. "I might have to." With a grin, he walked back over and sat behind his desk again.

Brent came back in and looked from one to the other. Reid had a hard time keeping a straight face when his partner's eyes were filled with questions.

Jacinda smiled at him. "Did you find anything out from Ms. Thomas's accountant?"

He handed her the cup. "Nothing too interesting, unless you like numbers. The financial statements are in the folder, other than a few bad investments, there's nothing."

"Mmm." She sipped the tea and then smiled at him again. "Thanks." Getting up she wandered over to the table that seemed to be growing with papers but no answers. "I'm just going to take a read through it and see if anything pops out at me."

Brent set the cup on his partner's desk. "A neon sign giving up the killers name would be great."

She laughed. "I don't see things in that sort of way, Brent, sorry."

He shrugged. "Was worth a try."

Reid watched her read through the reports. She was chewing her lip again. Every time he saw her do that, he wanted to stand ready with his gun and search, he smirked. Probably because every time she did that, whether she realized it or not, she found something.

He sat back, glancing over at his partner. From the way Brent was watching her, he also felt that anticipation when Jacinda was studying things.

Jac looked up at him suddenly. "Web businesses are almost as pricey as real ones." She glanced back down to the pages in her hand. "There are three rather large amounts that have been given to Edward Lawson of Love Quest dating in the last two months."

Reid pulled out his notebook as he got up. He looked over her shoulder as she pointed out the amounts to him. "We'll be sure to ask Mr. Lawson why that much and what exactly it was used for."

Brent sighed. "See, now she's cheating, I didn't know the name of the owners when I got that."

Jac looked over and grinned at him. "Well, there is another name that's jumping out at me. Do you want to check into it?"

He nodded and got up to get the papers from her. She pointed out the name to him. He smiled and looked down at her. "No neon sign though?" She shook his head. "Oh well, I prefer the old-fashioned way."

Reid laughed. "I prefer any way that gives us this guy."

~

By the time it was time for them to go to the meeting Jac was happy to get out from in front of the computer. She'd looked at almost every male profile from Love Quest and she was so tired of seeing faces inside a blue heart frame.

Climbing into the car with Reid, she turned to tell him she never wanted to look at another dating profile again when he reached over and pulled her closer to him. Before she could say a word his mouth came down on hers and every thought she had in her head was gone.

When he lifted his head, she smiled at him. "That is so much nicer than you growling at me."

He grinned. "I don't growl."

She leaned forward a few inches and lightly kissed him. "Yes, you do."

He hesitated for a moment as if he was going to kiss her again but straightened away from her. He studied her for a moment. "If something doesn't happen with this case today, I will be growling a lot." He bared his teeth at her playfully.

She laughed. "Let's just get there, I'm curious to see what these men are going to say when we tell them what's going on."

~

Mrs. Oster smiled over at them again. "It's going to be a little while more." She grimaced. "They're a bit behind today."

Reid shrugged. "That's fine, we'll wait." Really, he had no choice. He wasn't sure what he was hoping for here, but if it turned up anything further, it would be better than the walls they had been slamming into one after the other.

She smiled. "Okay good, because you really have to put a stop to all this, it's just awful."

Reid nodded. "Oh, we will get to the bottom of it." He looked down at Jac and smirked. Mrs. Oster still believed the motive was an STI and neither of them wanted to frighten her by telling her otherwise.

Jac sighed and glanced at the clock. She had already looked through most of the magazines on the table, he doubted if she read anything in the choices there. It was now three twenty and he was getting antsy.

Jac got up and went over to the desk. "Is there a bathroom I could use?"

Mrs. Oster smiled and pointed down the hall. "First door."

"Thank you." Jac wandered down the hallway and went in.

Reid turned from the odd painting; he'd been studying off and on since they'd got here, to see Jacinda come walking quickly towards him. She sat down sideways on the chair. Her face was pale and she was shaking.

She leaned closer to him and whispered. "Reid, I just saw him."

He gave her a puzzled look. "What like a flashback?"

She shook her head quickly and took a shaky breath. "No. He just went down the hall and around the corner." She hissed. She placed a shaking hand on his leg. "I can't be here."

His whole body went tense. He took her hand and stood up. He smiled over at the older woman behind the desk. "We're just going to go down to that little café and get a drink."

She nodded and smiled sweetly at them. "I'm sure you'll be back in plenty of time." She winked at him. "I'll stall them if you aren't."

"Thank you." He said quickly as he hugged Jac under his arm. When they were out of sight, he stopped and looked down at her. "Are you sure?" Her whole body was quaking as she nodded. "Okay." He rubbed his hands up and down her arms a few times then hugged her to him for a moment. "Let's get you out of here and get Brent."

She nodded again and walked tight against his side. She kept taking deep breaths and he tried to stay calm. His first priority was to get her to safety. Nothing could happen to Jacinda, to do otherwise was not an option.

He pulled his phone out and hit a button. Walking quickly, he kept her tight against him as he constantly scanned every person they saw. "He's in this building. She saw him in a hallway. How far away are you? Where is everyone else?" He nodded. "Call Alec and see if she's close by. I'm putting her in the car. Be here in five or less." He hung up the phone, stuffing it back in his pocket. He looked down at her, she was even paler. "Hey, it's okay. We've got him." She looked up at him and nodded as the elevator opened.

Moving quickly, he got her through the lobby and out to his car. Opening it he gently nudged her into the passenger seat.

He kissed her lightly on the mouth a few times, and then squatted down beside her. "I'll wait here until Brent gets here."

"I'm sorry," she whispered.

He looked at her for a second. "Don't be. I wouldn't expect you to be able to be near someone that has done something like that." He kissed her quickly again, as he spotted Brent running across the street.

He straightened. "Close the door, lock it and stay here."

She nodded and did exactly what he had told her to do.

~

Brent took the stairs two at a time trying to keep up with his partner. When they got to the top of the stairs, he grabbed his arm. "Jac going to be all right?"

Reid nodded briskly. "Yeah, it just scared her half to death, almost coming face to face with him."

"Can't blame her there." Brent took a deep breath and then motioned towards the office doors. "Let's get it done."

They both spun around when the elevator opened, and Detective Alec stepped out. The tall blonde smirked at them before her face went deadly serious and she pulled the gun from her jacket. "Let's play, boys."

Reid shook his head as he looked back towards the office door. With his hand on his gun, he pushed the door open. Mrs. Oster looked frozen in her chair and he couldn't blame her there, the three of them standing shoulder to shoulder made one hell of a fierce-looking wall. "Which office?" He asked her quietly. She pointed down the hallway that Jac had gone down.

"End on the left."

He nodded and motioned to Mrs. Oster as Brent headed towards the hall. "Go over and stay in that corner out of the way." He made sure she'd moved before he followed his partner.

When they reached the door, he looked back to see Alec standing like an amazon warrior by the end of the hall. Personally, if he were a criminal, he'd just give up the minute he encountered that cop. There wasn't a nice, compassionate bone in her body.

"Ready?" Brent whispered.

He jerked his chin towards the door as his partner stood to the side and held his hand over the doorknob.

~

Sandy was waiting for them when they reached the station. She practically pulled Jac from Reid's car and shoved her into her own.

Jac didn't want to go in the building. Just following Brent and seeing that man in the back of his car was close enough for her. She could hardly remember any of the drive back to the station; she'd never felt so afraid before.

Reid held her hand all the way to the station. His emotions

were angrier than she had noticed before, but he was able to keep his concern for her strong, enough that his hand was more comforting to her than she could express. He didn't even get the chance to kiss her, as Sandy had whipped open the passenger door as soon as the car was stopped. He told her quickly he'd come to her place as soon as they wrapped things up and give her an update.

She had been drowning in tears by the time Sandy got her home. "Go take a hot shower and I'll put the kettle on." She hugged her again. "I can't believe what you've been putting yourself through lately."

Jac sniffled. "It's like all the tears I held back every day, while doing this, want out now."

Sandy nodded. "That's healthy, to a point. Now go drown some of it under hot water and we'll sit here and breathe a sigh of relief together when you're done."

Jac smiled. "Thanks."

18

Jac watched Sandy pace around the room again. "I think you're more anxious to find out what's been going on than I am."

Sandy stopped and looked at her. "Well, it's not every day my best friend helps to apprehend a killer."

"True. Don't get used to it though, this is the first, last, and only time." Jac looked at the clock again. Did it really take two hours to do whatever it was that had to be done when someone was arrested? "I don't even know who he was."

"Does it matter?" Sandy perched on the edge of the chair.

Jac thought. "Not really, just curious as to how, why, and everything." She bit her lip. "I have so many questions, yet at the same time, I don't want to know any more about it.

"Well, I for..." She stopped and looked at the door when someone knocked on it. "I'll get it."

Jac smiled, Sandy was at the door before she could even get to her feet. She stood there almost holding her breath as Reid walked in. He looked tired and frustrated.

Reid grinned at her. "Sorry for taking so long. Paperwork, which took some time to do, Brent and I needed to figure out small details." He smirked at her.

She raised an eyebrow. "Details that kept me out of it?"

He nodded and walked into the room. "Something like that." He dropped down into the chair and rubbed his hand down his face. "So, we arrested Alan Howard, processed him, and were halfway through a long discussion with him when his lawyer showed up." He shook his head. "Then we had to wait for their little meeting and then wait some more." He looked up at her still standing there not moving. "He confessed."

She let out a breath she'd been holding. "The owner of the dating site?" She frowned. "I didn't see that coming. Why?"

He threw up his hands. "We don't know yet, his lawyer wanted to confer with him some more, so any further discussions will have to wait until tomorrow. What we did find out was Ms. Thomas was not part of the plan though."

She sat down on the edge of the couch. "Why?" He shrugged. "Well, that would explain why I couldn't find him in the customer profiles." He nodded.

"And—more bonus points to you, we were in the middle of being told about how a promise of a winning trip was how he got them, but his lawyer arrived before we could get the details."

She chewed her lip. "That doesn't explain how the funds were transferred before they were killed though, it explains the clean clothes, but ..." She frowned. "How did his partner take it?"

Reid smirked. "His partner wasn't there at the time."

Sandy sat down and laughed. "Probably a good thing for him, I'd probably freak right out if you and your partner came barreling into my office."

He laughed. "I suppose." He gave Jac a serious look. "Brent is hanging around down there to see if anything else happens. He sent me to fill you in on what we know so far." He sat back suddenly and closed his eyes. She realized he ran on full speed while he was working a case, then probably crashed when it was over. "Hopefully tomorrow we'll get all the details, and everything will fall into place."

She nodded again. "Yeah, I guess one more night of wondering is okay as long as he's locked up."

"He won't be going anywhere for a long time. I'd be surprised if bail was even granted."

Sandy grimaced. "I hope it's not, people like that we don't need ..." Her beeper went off. "Uh. I'll be so happy when next week is here and I'm not on call." She stood up and sighed. "I want details in the morning."

Jac grinned at her. "Absolutely. Thanks for coming to rescue me."

Sandy grabbed her bag and shrugged. "I didn't mind at all, it saved me from a patient that just sits there and sighs for an hour at a time."

Jac grinned. "Well, as long as I was useful."

"Always are." She walked quickly to the door and waved with her cell phone in her hand. "Talk later."

Reid studied her for a moment. "Are you okay?"

Jac nodded. "Yes. I had a small emotional breakdown when we got here, I think it was mostly relief it was over, but I'm good now."

He gave her a sheepish grin. "I think Brent kicked me out because I was driving him crazy worrying about you."

"You didn't have to, I was fine." She hid how touched she was, especially when he had everything else to deal with.

"I couldn't help it. You were shaking when you walked back out into that waiting room…"

She clasped her hands and looked down at them. "Almost coming face to face with a man I saw almost felt…" She took a slow calming breath.

He moved quickly off the chair and knelt in front of her. Taking her clasped hands, he squeezed them in his own. "I didn't mean to drudge it back up."

She sat there looking at his hands holding hers. The fact that he could touch her, even though he'd just spent a few hours with a killer, and she could find no trace of it in his emotions. She smiled at him, searching the brilliant green of his eyes. "You have the most amazing control of your emotions Reid, it's like nothing I've ever experienced."

He watched her eyes. "It was a skill I had to acquire to survive what I do for a living."

"Hmm, and here I've always sought out intellectuals all my life, feeling they'd be in control. I never once thought I'd be able to be in the presence of anyone that dealt with the grim truth of humanity."

He dropped back onto his heels, studying her for a moment. "My ex couldn't handle what I dealt with; I tend to withdraw into myself sometimes."

"With good reason. I'm sure you see things that most people couldn't imagine." She sighed. "Withdrawing and staying inside of yourself is a coping technique people use without realizing it, or so

Sandy likes to keep telling me."

"Compared to what you have to live with every day, what I do seems easy."

Not knowing what else to do, she smiled shyly at him. Understanding wasn't something she was used to. She watched his eyes as his hand came to rest lightly against her cheek. She felt his strong fingers touch the back of her head. His eyes searched hers as he leaned closer to touch his lips against hers. The light touch of his mouth erased all the tension she'd been feeling. Resting her hand over his, she didn't want him to move away yet.

"Is my touch bothering you?" His voice was a whisper.

She shook her head.

Moving closer he turned his head and kissed her again. She returned the kiss, slowly taking her time to explore his mouth. He reached behind her, pulling her closer to the edge of the couch, so she could feel the heat from his body.

Needing the contact, she put her arms around his neck and pulled him against her. She wanted to feel the heat of his body against hers. She had been deprived of human contact most of her life, and here was a man that changed all the boundaries she'd needed, that allowed her to be able to be near someone. As his mouth moved across to her neck, she gasped. She leaned back further to give him access. The fire inside her burned hotter when he pulled her hips again and she slid off the couch to straddle his legs where he kneeled. The feel of his strong arms around her holding her tight against him made her feel dizzy.

The quiet gasps she was making as his mouth moved over her throat made him harder than he had been before. Reaching under her, he grasped the backs of her thighs, lifting her as he rose up to his knees. Her body brushing against him almost caused him to shake with a need he'd thought he'd never feel again.

Supporting her shoulders, he leaned her back on the couch and kneeled on one knee to look down at her. The hair she'd tried to secure was falling out and framing her face in gentle black wisps. Her eyes were clouded, lips swollen.

Reaching up she pulled the clip from her hair. She pushed herself to stretch out on the couch and reached up with a hand to pull on his shirt, bringing him back down to her. When he slowly lowered his body over hers, he could feel her heart beating as fast as his.

He held himself up on his elbows keeping most of his weight off her. She reached up with both hands she circled his neck, pulling his head down to hers. Leaning up to meet his mouth with her own, she whispered against it. "I haven't been close to anyone in a long time, Reid." She kissed softly beside his mouth, gazing up into his eyes.

The reality that she'd had a life starved of contact with others made the fact that he was with her right now even more important. He kissed one eyelid, then the other and watched her eyes slowly open. "Neither have I." He ran his tongue down the silky skin of her throat. "We'll take this slow." His body wasn't agreeing with his words, but he regained his control, determined to make sure he didn't rush this.

Her small hands worked his shirt out of his jeans. When her hot palms ran up his back, it felt like trails of fire everywhere she touched. She pushed his shirt up his back and began pulling it over his shoulders. Leaning up he pulled it free from his body and moved back down to her quickly.

Lost in the feelings she was creating and the feel of the warmth of her body, he felt like he was on fire and floating at the same time. Her hands moved over the bare skin on his chest, lifting her head her mouth followed them. Her tongue brushed over his skin and he need for her flared again. Reaching up she pulled his mouth down to hers once more.

Slipping his hand under her head he lifted her head and devoured her mouth, showing the hunger he felt for her. With every touch, his need became more undeniable. Resting his weight on the arm that held her head, he moved his other down to pull the shirt from her pants. Lifting his head, he moved down to run his mouth over her rib cage. With his teeth and free hand, he pulled the buttons open to expose her pale soft skin. Looking up at her flushed face, he ran his tongue slowly along the edge of the white lace bra she wore. Her mouth opened and gasped again.

He realized they were on the couch like a couple of teenagers. Running his tongue along the lace again he grinned when her hand tightened in his hair. "Let's take this into the other room." He didn't wait for a response, just slid up to his knees, lifting her with him. When she wrapped her legs around his waist, he wasn't sure if he'd be able to walk to the bedroom. When he stood to his full height, her body rested against the throbbing hard on in his pants.

Walking quickly towards the bedroom, he almost stumbled when her mouth moved up his neck, her legs tightening around him as she stretched up his body. Pausing, he leaned her against wall and grabbed the backs of her thighs to rub her body up and down the hard length of him while he kissed her with a need that left them both panting.

She leaned her head back against the wall, looking at him. "I think the time for slow has passed." She grinned at him as he nodded breathlessly, pulling her tight against his chest to walk the rest of the way to the bedroom.

Stopping beside the bed, he lowered her to stand and pulled her shirt off her arms. Nipping her neck gently he whispered against her ear. "These clothes need to go." His hands moved to the button on her pants and undid them.

She was only able to hang onto his neck to support her weight, trying to keep upright as his hands moved inside her pants to push them to the floor, as his mouth sucked along the edge of her bra. Dropping her head back, she hugged his head closer to her skin. His gentle hands moved up her back to release the clasp of her bra. With one hand he pulled it up her arms as his mouth closed over one sensitive nipple.

As soon as her hands were free from the bra straps, she dropped them down to pull at the button on his jeans. Pulling the zipper down, she shoved at the waist of his jeans quickly pushing them down over his hips. She grasped him in her hand and ran her hand slowly up the length of him. He grasped her hand to stop her. With quick moves, he got his wallet out and pulled the condom out of it. When he'd put it there earlier, he never thought he'd be using it this soon.

"Let me savor you a bit first, if you touch me, I'm going to lose it." He bit the side of her neck and followed it with a lick. Kicking his jeans off his legs as his mouth followed the curve of her neck and shoulders, he leaned her back onto the bed.

Pulling the pants off her legs, his mouth moved up her thighs and across her hip. She sucked in a breath. "Reid…" His tongue dipped into her belly button. Grasping his hair, she pulled gently trying to get him back up to her mouth. "I want you to…" His lips closed over her nipple and sucked hard on it. She tugged his hair again to be rewarded with his mouth on hers finally. Clinging to his neck she kissed him with the crazed need she was feeling. His hands shook as he put the protection on, he felt like he was fifteen all over again. Squirming, she moved under him completely and lifted herself until their bare bodies touched.

Groaning, he lifted his head and reached down to stroke a hand up the bare leg against his waist. Moving his hand under her, he lifted her hips and slowly slid into the tight, hot, heat waiting for him. He moved into her until their bodies were tight against each other. Running his hand down her leg he pulled out slowly again. Grasping behind her knee, pulling it higher, he moved into her slowly again. He could feel the strain already as he grit his teeth, lost in the amazing feeling of being inside her.

Jac moaned in the back of her throat, and then gasped and dropped her head back as he moved into her again. She tried to move to speed things up, but he held her so she was unable to do more, other than let him drive her into a slow torturous wantonness. He lowered his head and sucked a nipple into his mouth as he moved back into her, harder this time. She gasped, sucking in a breath. She wrapped the leg that was free around him and pulled him down towards her.

Lifting his head, he looked down into her eyes. The raw need he saw there was his undoing, releasing her knee he allowed her to move with him. Grasping her hip, he pulled her with more force against his body as he stroked into her. He cradled her head with his other hand, wanting to see her face.

She lifted her hips into his body. He knew she was on the edge, with each stroke he kept her just hovering there. Running her hands down his back, she pulled him harder into her body. His mouth rained hard kisses against her throat as he moved into her. The rhythm was getting faster with each stroke.

When she started panting, he lifted his head, watching her face as she went over the edge. Just watching her made him lose that last thread of control he had, a fire moved through his whole being. He thrust into her again and felt her muscles contracting around him. Dropping his head, he gasped into her ear. "Jacinda." Then he crashed over the edge with her.

Panting to catch his breath, he focused on keeping his body from dropping on her. Lifting his weight onto both arms, he slid them up beside her head, kissing his way across her shoulder. His arms began shaking, so he quickly flipped them so he was on his back. Blowing out a deep breath, he grinned into the hair that was surrounding him. Pulling the black silk away from his face he stroked a hand down her damp back. "I'm going to need a few to regroup before I continue that savoring part."

Smiling, she panted out a breath and lifted her head to look up at him. "Continue?" She grinned. "Again?" He felt his body stir inside hers and she laughed.

"Yeah." He said as he brushed the hair away from her face. Her dark eyes were still glazed. She laughed again. Grasping her hips, he pulled free from her warm body and moved her up to rest her head against his shoulder. Turning his head, he kissed her lingeringly. "If that's okay with you that is." He whispered against her mouth.

She smirked contently. "Oh, I think it will be."

19

Brent burned his tongue on his coffee the next morning when Reid came in later than ever. He assumed his partner was already downstairs. He watched Reid saunter, in that long stride of his, over to the coffee. When his partner patted him on the back and said "morning", Brent was sure his jaw must have dropped. Smirking, he watched him make his coffee. Was he humming under his breath? Reid? He cleared his throat. "I don't know who you are, but I have a gun and will find out what you've done with that miserable cuss of a partner of mine."

Reid laughed then took a sip of his coffee. "I can assure you I'm still your miserable cuss of a partner." He shook his head, walking away still grinning.

Brent stood there and watched him greet a few other people before he headed down the stairs. "The hell you are." He said quietly to himself then followed him down.

Reid sat behind his desk with his feet up on the corner looking over a report sheet as he sipped his coffee.

Brent leaned in the doorway and watched him. "So, how was Jac doing yesterday?"

He didn't glance up from the report. "She was just fine when I got there, the doc stayed with her."

Brent took another sip of his coffee. "And how was she doing this morning?" He grinned.

Reid glanced at him over the top of the papers and grinned.

"Just fine."

"Uh huh, I knew it was either her or you'd taken up drinking."

Reid laughed. "You're a great detective." He looked at the clock. "What time is his lawyer due to be here?"

"About now."

Reid dropped his feet to the floor and stood up. "Let's go have a chat with them."

Brent watched him saunter out of the office and shook his head grinning as he followed him. About time some woman put a smile on his grouchy face.

~

Jac opened the office door, trying not to drop the bags she carried. Bumping it closed with her hip she set the bags on the table and shrugged out of her jacket. Her whole body ached, but in a completely delicious way. She caught her reflection in the window and grinned. "Don't you look like a happy one today." The phone rang. Still grinning she answered. "Jacinda Brown."

"I have this bed I need you to check out, Jacinda Brown."

She grinned at Reid's playful tone. "Oh really? Is it old?"

"Not very."

"Hmm, does it have a lot of history?" She tried to sound serious.

"None at all."

She smiled. "I don't understand what I can do for you then, sir."

Reid cleared his throat. "Help me make some history in it, after dinner."

She laughed. "I would love to, help you that is." She perched on the edge of her desk. "Aren't you supposed to be working, Detective?"

He sighed, "just waiting for his lawyer to come out, so we can go in."

"Ah." She pushed the hair from her face.

"My cell number come up on your phone?"

She glanced down. "Yes."

"Put it in yours and let me know later what time we'll meet for dinner."

She smiled again. "Okay. Now, go do your mean cop thing."

"Who says I'm the mean one?"

She laughed. "Just a lucky guess."

He laughed. "I didn't want to leave this morning."

She blushed. "I didn't want you to."

"Then why aren't we still there?"

She laughed again. "Work, the real world, and all that."

"Right. Okay, beautiful I'll talk to you later." He paused. "Oh, Brent needs to speak to you later he says, something about you replacing his miserable cuss of a partner with some happy guy."

She blushed. "You can just tell him I'll talk to him later so he can thank me."

"Will do. Bye."

"Bye." She hung up the phone still laughing. She never would have guessed he had a silly side. It was a pleasant surprise.

Sighing Jac surveyed the office. "Okay, time to get you sorted out and cleaned up, then maybe I will try to be here more." Picking up the hair clip on her desk, she quickly twisted her hair up out of the way.

Grinning, she pulled her phone out of her purse and quickly entered Reid's number. She'd have to make sure she gave herself enough time to go home and get cleaned up before their dinner.

Setting the phone down she glared at the windows. Clean windows would make a good start. Reaching into the bags she began pulling out the cleaning products.

Jac gave the desk one final push then huffed out a breath. Shoving the stray hairs back off her face, she went over and got a bottle of water from the small fridge.

Taking a few cooling mouths full as she looked around the room she smiled. "I think I might be winning."

The whole room had been re-arranged. She could now sit at her desk and look out her clean windows to see the world. Okay, the world stopped at the corner, but that was good too.

Sitting down, she looked at the clock. Picking up her cell phone she grinned. She was anxious for the day to end. She'd be able to find out the details from Reid tonight and that she was seeing Reid tonight.

Opening his number to send him a text, she chewed her lip. How long would he be at the station? Was six too early?

She heard her office door open. You forgot to lock the door, ninny, she silently chastised. Turning her head, she pasted a smile on her face. "Sorry we're not…" She dropped the phone on the desk and sat there staring at the man as he closed the door and leaned against it. It was Alan Howard.

"I can tell by the look on your face, you're making the same mistake as everyone else." He stood there with his hands tucked into his jacket pockets. "I'm Edward Lawson. Al is my cousin." He smirked. "I usually wear ugly eyeglasses to make us look different."

Her heart felt like it was in her throat. "Oh." She put a hand on her chest trying to will herself to calm down. "What can I do for you?" He stood there smiling at her. Every nerve in her body was going off at the same time, something wasn't right. Why didn't he explain why he was here? He took two steps towards her, she glanced at the door as she slowly stood up, hoping she'd make it if she tried.

"I'd like to know how you did it."

She watched, waiting for him to move away from the door. "Did-did what?" When he smiled at her again a strange look appeared in his eyes.

"How did you do it?" He stepped closer, still blocking the door. "How did you trace it back to us?" He lifted his hands out of his pockets.

Her throat began to hurt when she saw the knife in his hand. "Who?" She croaked.

Anger appeared in his eyes. "No one knows computer trails like Alan. He was working on figuring out how you did it, while I got the money and closed the bank account. I was supposed to open another account; we knew not to use them for too long."

Pieces flew together inside her mind suddenly. "Who told you I knew anything?"

He gave her a disgusted look. "Mrs. Oster bought your story hook, line and sinker." He snarled. "Stupid bitch should have told us who we were meeting yesterday, and we would have disappeared forever instead of being there."

She had to do something to distract him then maybe she could get closer to the door. "Your plan was nearly flawless." She said it quietly trying to hide the fear in her voice.

He studied her silently for a moment then grinned. "Yeah, it was. Where did we trip up?"

She tried to focus on keeping her breathing steady. "Ms. Thomas."

He frowned. "Al was right."

He paced a few feet to the left; she almost had a clear shot at the door.

"I wasn't supposed to kill her. Al was pissed. I was just supposed to drug her enough to get her flown somewhere out of the way."

Jac licked her dry lips. "Why did you?" He waved his hand around as he talked; she tried not to look at the knife flashing in the light as he did.

"Mrs. Oster confided in Dawn about your little disease tale, and she was getting bitchy." He frowned. "She was all for it until she thought we might get caught, then she wouldn't shut up about it." He shrugged. "So, I killed her. We could have done more and been living on some nice tropical island by now." He snarled at her. "If it hadn't been for you sticking your nose in."

He took a few steps towards her and she felt her knees begin to quake.

"Do you have any idea how many selfish women I had to pretend to care about? Each one took weeks of chatting and stupid coffee dates…"

She willed her mind to find something to keep him talking. "I never—I didn't figure out how you …"

He grinned again. "Oh, you wouldn't find our profiles or us on any list contacting other members. Al was really good at making us vanish in between." He bowed in a sarcastic manner. "In my profile I'm Eddie Black. Al was Albert White." He moved another step closer. "We used older pictures even if you had been looking when our profiles were visible; I doubt you would have recognized us." He smirked.

She took a small step backwards and found her legs against the other desk, having forgotten she'd moved it earlier. "How-how did you talk them into giving you money?" Her heart was now pounding in her ears so loudly she wasn't sure she was going to be able to stay calm much longer.

He gave a strangled laugh. "Stupid bitches fell for the whole thing." He stepped closer, looking down at her and sneered. "Their greed and they wanted to be the one to help the computer genius, whose grant money had run out, finish his project and be a part of the new generation of computers." He laughed again. "I spent hours using lines Al had written down for me to impress them, still have no clue what I was actually saying in English." He stopped and studied her.

She could feel the sweat running down the back of her neck, she took a few short breaths trying to find something else to ask him. "So-so Alan killed them all…"

He laughed. "Al killed the first one, then couldn't do the rest." He sneered at her. "He was there when I did it each time, to help get them changed and get rid of any prints, but he really didn't have the stomach for the dirty parts."

He'd moved closer again and she studied his face. His anger was growing. "Oh. Oh, well you definitely kept the police w-wondering." She tried to swallow but her throat was too dry. As he moved closer, she leaned back to rest her hands on the desk; her knees were threatening to give out at any moment. He stopped inches from her then stood there looking at her. She couldn't define the expression in his eyes. Her hands were starting to shake, and she silently prayed he wouldn't touch her.

He grasped her shoulder and squeezed it. "We did." He said quietly. "Until you came along." He snarled. "How the hell did you get brought in?"

His anger radiated into her system. She gripped the desk harder trying to focus on staying above the vile emotions flooding into her. "Elaine, I…" She tried to swallow again. "I knew Elaine."

He released her shoulder and smiled. "Elaine had brains." He frowned. "I almost liked her." He stood there quietly for a moment. "She asked questions, thought she was going with me to see my working prototype…" He shook his head and studied her again.

Jac felt the bottle by her hand and hoped it was the window cleaner. If she could just get to the door… The phone rang making her jump. She stared at it as it continued to ring. He didn't look at it once, just continued to stand there and leer at her. He moved suddenly, grabbing her wrist, pulling her hand away from the bottle.

"Don't be stupid." He said his face only an inch from hers.

She bit her lip, hoping the pain would help her focus as she tried not to collapse on the floor. His bare hand touching her wrist filled her head with images. If he was feeling anything but hate, she couldn't find it. Looking up into his face, still a breath away from hers, she grasped the desk with her other hand and leaned back from him. He lifted the hand with the knife in it right in front of her face. Her stomach lurched from the disturbing images he projected inside her.

"Now, what to do with you." He mused quietly.

His voice faded when he spoke as she fought to stay conscious. She had to be alert and fight this. She could hear her cell phone vibrating across the desk and hoped it was someone on the other end that would somehow know she was in trouble.

"You ruined everything…" The phone on the desk started ringing again. He pushed her towards the desk. "Answer it so I can think."

She rested both hands on her desk, breathing, trying to focus on the phone. He moved to stand right behind her.

"Not a word. Don't be stupid." He hissed into her ear.

She grabbed at the phone twice before she was able to pick it up.

"Jac? Where were you?"

Sandy's voice echoed in her ear. "I was," she took a deep breath. It was hard to speak with him so close to her. The hand with the knife came around her head to hover right in front of her face. "Moving desk," she gasped out.

Sandy laughed. "Sounds more like you were trying to bench press it. Sit down and catch your breath."

His mouth touched her other ear. "Get rid of them."

"Have to," she stared at the knife moving closer, "finish." She whispered.

"Hmm, I was looking for details woman. How was your night after I left?"

She swallowed again. "I—*Brent* was amazing." She said it quickly as the knife rested against the mouthpiece of the phone. "Have to go." Quickly she hung up. She stood there unable to make her body move. He grasped her wrist and spun her around to face him. She felt the edge of the desk against her hip, but wasn't able to focus on anything other than his emotions.

"Good girl."

His voice sounded hallow. She had to focus. Had to stay awake until someone came. She started to feel cold and knew the shaking would start soon.

"You need to calm down."

His image was a blur when she tried to look at him, making her feel even more lightheaded. He pushed her arm behind her back and leaned into her. She could feel his breath on her face, and it made her head spin. The pain flooded into her stomach, she twitched, trying to bend forward to ease it.

"What the hell is wrong with you? Are you having some sort of seizure or something?" He pulled her upright and grasped her face. "Don't make me have to carry you out of here."

She couldn't make out any of the words he was saying. She could barely focus enough to identify the cool steel of the blade touching her cheek as he held her chin. She tired breathing in through her nose to climb out away from the unconsciousness that was looming towards her. She focused on opening her eyes but couldn't. Reid …

She didn't know where she was. She knew she was horizontal but felt like she was floating somewhere. She could hear footsteps and shuffling. She could smell something awful, and it made her stomach heave. The pain wouldn't last much longer she thought, almost relieved. Just breathe. She thought she felt someone moving her but couldn't hear anything now. Just rest her mind told her. Rest.

~

Reid glanced again in the mirror at the doctor. "Has she moved at all?" She shook her, head. "Are you sure we should take her home?"

Sandy nodded again. "I am not taking her to a hospital. Do you have any idea what they'd do to her if they knew or even if they knew and didn't believe her?" She shook her head again and reached out to stroke a hand down Jac's cheek. "Jacinda? Jac? Come on, just open your eyes and let me know you're in there." She glanced at him in the mirror again. "I've never been unable to get her to surface, even a little."

He looked in the mirror, and then quickly back to the road. He didn't like the sounds of that. "We're almost there, we'll get her inside and see if we can rouse her at all, if not I'm calling someone for help."

Sandy looked down at her friend then back to the mirror. She nodded.

20

Jac opened her eyes. They felt gritty. Her tongue was so dry it hurt. Turning her head, she tried to focus. She was in her bedroom. A dream? Was that just some dream? She looked at the clock. Three ten. She closed her eyes and tried to remember coming home and going to bed. Opening them again, she looked around in the dark. There were cups on the table. More nightmares. She should have known.

Letting her eyes droop closed again, she took a few long deep breaths and tried to force her head to remember the events that led up to her being here again. She smirked. Since when was it her fault she was like this? Okay, so sometimes she didn't walk away when she really should. Running her hands over her face she stopped. She had a, what was it? A band-aid was on her cheek? She frowned. How did that happen? What was going on?

Flipping the covers off, she slowly pushed herself up. Her arms were shaking. The room spun a few times, stopping she just sat there trying to breathe through it. She thought she heard someone talking. Where were those voices coming from? She squeezed her head between her hands. That's new, hearing voices. Maybe she was finally going nuts, it had felt like it many times in her life. She sighed, realizing it was probably just Sandy babysitting her, staying awake by watching the TV.

Slowly, she moved to hang her legs off the bed. She wasn't sure if she was even going to be able to stand. But with her throat so dry she couldn't call Sandy for help. Looking over she reached with a heavy, shaking arm to see if there was any sort of liquid left in either of the cups. They were empty. Great. She stopped and wondered for a moment if people put little water coolers beside the bed, it was a perfect spot for one. Shaking her head, she huffed out a breath. What was wrong with her brain?

An inch at a time she pushed herself to the edge of the bed. Maybe she should buy herself a walker for moments like this. She grinned, despite the fog plaguing her head; she was not buying a walker.

Pushing herself to her feet, she stood there with wobbling knees and her whole body shaking. Her legs felt like lead as she took the first step. Panting out a breath she reached out to steady herself against the wall. Okay, she could do this. Another step. She wasn't sure if she was lifting her foot or dragging it, but as long as she moved forward, that was just fine.

It felt like it took her an hour to get halfway down the short hallway. She debated for a few moments on whether sitting on the floor to rest was a good idea. With the way her body felt, she was afraid she'd never get back off the floor. Then she'd be left there until Sandy came to check on her again. What if Sandy had fallen asleep? No, sitting was a bad idea. Standing there she rested her forehead and both hands against the wall. Take a minute, regroup she told herself silently.

"Don't you know any doctor friends that could come here?"

That was Reid's voice.

"She would never forgive any of us."

That was Sandy. Right Sandy, no doctors.

"Reid, just give her body some time to rest."

Brent. Brent was here too? When was this?

"She's been resting for almost twelve hours now, other than waking up a few times she just lies there!"

Twelve hours? That was record. What had she done to put herself under for twelve hours? Why wasn't her brain giving her answers?

"Reid…"

"She doesn't speak, just drinks that tea and has this empty look in her eyes, like she's not there."

Reid sounded really upset. What was wrong with her? She slid, with her shoulder resting against the wall a few more steps.

Even her shoulders began to feel leaden, her arms suddenly feeling removed from her body. She lowered her eyes to the floor, either she wasn't moving her feet, or she was sliding down the wall. She focused on the corner. It was getting closer; she just hoped she didn't reach it face first because she honestly, she didn't think she had the strength to lift her own arms to stop a fall.

She barely reached the corner when she saw Reid running towards her.

"Jacinda." He got to her as she slid down the wall. Scooping her up against his chest, he quickly walked to the couch. "What are you doing up?" He sat down still holding her against him.

She looked up at him and smiled. "Out of body experience." She whispered hoarsely.

Sandy hovered above her and held out a bottle of water. She wanted that water like she hadn't had a drink in a week, but her arms were imaginary and weren't really attached to her body. Sandy grinned at her, and then knelt holding the open bottle by her mouth. Swallowing hurt, but the cool water felt so good. "Thanks." She looked back up at the man holding her. His eyes were darting over her face, a mix of concern and relief swimming in them. She smiled at him. "I'm missing a few details here."

He rested his forehead against hers. "You scared the hell out of me."

Jac smiled at him again. "I seem to be good at that." Brent moved into her view and stood above her.

"Maybe you could let her stretch out on the couch Reid."

She smirked at the snarl Reid gave his partner. Brent held up his hands and backed away. Reid looked back down at her and sighed. With a sigh, he shifted so she was lying back on the cushions and he was sitting on the edge of the couch. Sandy reappeared with a cup in her hand. "Uh, not the tea."

Sandy smirked. "Yes, the tea. You drink it; we'll fill in the details."

Jac moaned. "Just set it down and give me a minute." Closing her eyes, she took a few breaths. A cool hand moved across her forehead and down her cheek. The touch she knew. She opened her eyes to look at Reid. She didn't need ask if it had been rough for her, she could feel it in his shaking hand. His thumb stroked over the band-aid. "Let's start with that." She said to him quietly. "Where did that come from?"

He looked down at her for a moment and then sighed again. Standing up he paced to the end of the couch. "That came from Edward Lawson's knife as you passed out and slid to the floor."

The images and memories flooded into her mind all at once. She hugged her arms against her stomach. "It really happened." He nodded with his jaw set. Even though everything was cloudy inside her, it didn't go unnoticed that he had moved away from her to discuss this. She looked at Brent. "Did I at least pass out gracefully?"

Brent smirked, and then caught the glare from his partner. "You passed out right as Reid barreled through the office door and almost gave Mr. Lawson a coronary."

"Ah." She looked to Reid again. "Do I have to buy a new office door?"

Reid looked at her for a moment and then shrugged. "It's still intact, just needs a new handle and lock."

"Well." Blowing out a breath, she looked at Sandy. "You called the cavalry for me?"

Sandy nodded. "After I stood there for half a second wondering what drugs you were taking. They were already on route when I called though."

Jac gave Reid a puzzled look.

"We had just heard the entire story from Alan Howard when I received your blank text message. When I called you didn't answer," he stuffed his hands in his pockets. "If we hadn't gotten stuck behind an accident, we would have been there sooner..."

"He was ready to run there on foot." Brent added in. "I was waiting for him to bolt out of the car.

She chewed her lip. "So, Alan told you about Edward, the profiles and..."

Reid nodded. "Everything." He sat on the edge of the couch again. "He left out the part where they knew about you until the very last."

"Which would be perfectly timed to your blank message." Brent gave her a serious look. "When Doctor Gains' call was put through to Reid's cell phone, *I* was ready to run there on foot."

She smiled at him. "Well." She let out the breath she'd been holding. She closed her eyes for a moment, letting the relief wash over her. The satisfying feeling that she had done something good, something right. Regardless of what people thought of her or the freaky ability she'd been blessed, or cursed with, this feeling made it all worth it. It made all the rest easy to store away for a while, to a place she never willingly went on her own. She opened her eyes and looked at Reid again. "Case closed."

Sandy picked up the cup again. Jac moaned. "Fine." She pushed herself up with numb arms and reached to slowly take the cup. The liquid in it sloshed around the rim. "I'm a little hungry." She said as she focused on getting the cup to her mouth.

"I'll go make some oatmeal." Sandy stood up.

"I'm going to go home and grab a few seconds of sleep before I have to be awake again." Brent stood up. He nodded to Jac. "Try to behave."

She sipped the tea slowly, glancing momentarily towards Reid, and then smirked at Brent. "Like I have a choice right now."

Reid stood there looking down at her. She was white. She was shaking. But she was awake. "You added ten years to my age today, yesterday."

She set the cup down, leaning back to look up at him. "That's good, now you're older than me." She smirked.

He sighed and sat down on the edge of the couch. "I'm serious, when I suspected something was wrong, I was just determined to get there quickly." He gently brushed the hair back from her face. "When Sandy called—I have never been so scared in my life, Jacinda." He leaned down and rested his forehead against hers. "Don't ever do that again."

She had never had the feeling of really mattering to someone before, but it flooded into her with his words alone. She saw the love in his eyes and felt it burst through her. Just feeling it was more than she'd ever allowed herself to hope for. Reaching up she wrapped her arms around his neck and cradled his head. "It wasn't exactly intentional, believe me. But I am definitely sticking to furniture from now on."

He grinned. "Please." Lifting his head and looked down at her, the hard look in his eyes softening. "I took a few days off, so you can take your time recovering."

She raised her eyebrows looking back at him. "You're staying to babysit me for a few days?"

He nodded. "For my own benefit more than yours. I've decided I'm not letting you out of my sight again. Ever."

She smirked. "That's going to make working rather difficult…" His mouth covered hers before she could finish speaking. Gently his lips moved over hers. She closed her eyes and let the emotion he was feeling poor into her. She had never felt so cherished, and he gave that to her.

"Do you think limiting her oxygen supply right now will help her recovery?"

Reid lifted his head and grinned while still looking at Jacinda. "Probably not, but if I keep her weak enough, she can't give me gray hair."

Sandy laughed. "Why do you think mine is more dye than natural blonde now? Keeping up with Jacinda Brown is a full-time occupation."

Jac's mouth dropped open as she pushed Reid, barely moving him. "Jacinda Brown is right here people, can we not talk like she isn't?"

Reid sat up and laughed. "You just listen to the doctor and eat your oatmeal; I'm going to pop home and grab some things."

Jac frowned at him. "She's a head doctor."

"Hey." Sandy stood above her grimacing. "I'm the only doctor you have, so you'd better listen."

"Fine." She held up her hands in defeat. She watched as Reid almost ran from the room, and then turned to Sandy.

Sandy was standing there smirking at her. "Eat your oatmeal before I get all sappy or something."

Jac laughed and sat up a bit further. "Absolutely, the last thing I need is a sappy head doctor on my hands."

Sandy sat silently watching her for a few moments. "I'm going to take advantage of your being weak." She smirked. "I just spent twelve hours watching that man …" She pointed to the door Reid had gone out. "Losing his mind worrying over you, so you owe me a few tidbits." She grinned when Jac rolled her eyes at her. "I'm not asking for intimate details, just how it is."

Jac paused and put the spoon down. "It's wonderful." She smiled. "He can just shut off all emotion, Sandy, and to me that's amazing." Sandy's eyebrows went up. "I know your education says that's all bad, but to me it's a miracle."

Sandy pursed her lips for a moment. "I suppose it would be." Sighing she leaned back and rubbed her tired eyes. "I'd just like to see you happy."

Jac smirked. "I am. I'm not saying this is happily-ever-after, I won't put that on either of us, but I am happy."

Sandy just sat back and smiled at her. "It's about time."

They both laughed.

21

Jacinda rolled over and lifted her head and looked at the sleepy man beside her. "What do you mean the Captain wants to see me?" She frowned. "Why?"

Reid grinned as he ran a hand down her disheveled hair. "He called me last night and said to see if you would come in today sometime."

She chewed her lip. "And you're just telling me now?"

He shrugged and leaned over to kiss her bare shoulder. "I meant to tell you, then you came out of the bathroom in a towel." He kissed the side of her neck. "A towel—how is that playing fair? I'm supposed to be looking after you while you recover."

She pushed him onto his back. "It had been two days, I was recovered." She sat up and glared down at him. "You need to get ready for work." Turning, she swung her legs over the side of the bed.

He reached out, wrapping his arm around her waist and pulled her back into the bed. "And where do you think you're going?"

She laughed, trying to pry the arm off her waist. "To shower."

He kissed the back of her neck and then let her go. "Well, that's fine then, proceed." He flipped the sheet off and grinned as he climbed out of the bed behind her. "You can wash my back, I'll wash yours."

She turned around and held the robe she'd been trying to find the sleeve on against her. "You'll get my hair wet, it takes forever to dry, Reid."

He stood there naked and shook his head. "I won't get it wet." He winked at her and pulled the robe from her hands, tossing it to the floor. He scooped her up into his arms as she shrieked. "We'll get it wet."

~

She'd promised Reid she would only be an hour behind him. At the time she'd meant it too. But Sandy had called her, so she went there first. She chewed her lip as she drove the last few blocks to the station. The whole situation Sandy had described had her a little more than concerned. She had that feeling again, the one that told her something wasn't right.

Sandy asking her to dig up stuff on someone was just a little more than odd; she'd never done that before. Was it because it was a person, and until recently she didn't do people? Jac wanted to think that was it, but something told her the whole thing was unusual enough to have Sandy worried. Hopefully Reid and Brent wouldn't mind her cheating and using their databases to get this quickly for her.

Once she was inside the building, she quickly headed down towards the basement office.

People smiled at her along the way, being used to her coming and going now she supposed. Jac still didn't feel comfortable enough to pause long enough to converse with anyone. Being around people was still something that was too new to her. Someday soon— maybe she could try.

Her nerves were so unsettled today, she still wasn't sure why the Captain wanted her here, that added to the talk with Sandy had her jumpy. The heels she wore clicked on the floor, even though she was trying to walk softly. She wasn't even sure why she'd felt the urge to wear a skirt today. She smirked. Okay, so she wanted to look good for Reid.

Stopping at the bottom of the stairs she stood there for a second. She could not remember another time in her life she had dressed to look good for someone else. Grinning at that realization, she walked in the door.

Brent looked up from the papers he was studying. He whistled, making Reid immediately turn and snarl at him. Brent grinned. "Hey, no biting."

Reid sat back, watching her walk across the room towards him. Those sexy stocking clad legs demanded all his attention. He took his time looking over every inch of her, then up to her beautiful face. He smiled and received a smile, a blushing smile in return. "That was some long hour."

She frowned. "You noticed?"

Brent laughed and received another glare. "I think he looked at the clock and the door every two minutes, at least." He received a third glare. Smiling, he sat back.

Reid watched her chew her lip. "What's wrong?"

She leaned against her hip against his desk and shrugged. "I had to go see Sandy, she has a new patient, which has been forced by some judge to see her, so she wants me to dig around a bit for her. She's never asked me to do that before."

His brows furrowed. "By a judge?"

Jac nodded. "I'm a little sketchy on the details, and Sandy was not exactly calm in explaining the whole story to me. I'm not sure if it's because she was basically ordered to do this, or if she's really worried about the person. Can I run the name through here?"

Reid nodded. "Yeah, if the Doc is worried about it, you should check it out for her."

She grinned. "Thanks."

Brent cleared his throat. "Give me the name and I'll get started while you go talk to Cap."

She pulled a notebook from her purse, flipping it open she handed it to him. "Felicity Dante." She grinned at him. "Thanks." She looked at Reid. "You are coming with me?"

He smirked. "Yeah." He stood up.

Brent winked at Jac. "Relax, Cap doesn't bite."

She moved into his arm when he stood in front of her. "I'm not worried; if he gets mean Reid will shoot him."

Brent laughed. "Scary part is he just might."

Reid looked from one to the other. "Why do you two think I go around shooting people?" He looked down to see Jacinda laughing at him. Lowering his head, he kissed her hard then patted her butt. "Let's go."

He almost had to drag her along with him. The Captain had better just be wanting to say thank you to her. Reid really wasn't sure how he'd feel if it was more than that. He was certain though, that she would not be hunting down murderers – ever again! Anyone that so much as thought it would be answering to him.

Brent glanced up as they came back into the room a half hour later. "So, what's up?"

Reid smirked. "The department offered Jacinda the opportunity to do research for us." He gave her a serious look. "Just research." Jac smirked at him and nodded.

Brent raised his eyebrows.

Reid nodded. "I'm going to say William Azaire's influence is in there somewhere."

Brent nodded slowly. "Cool."

Jac sat on the edge of the desk and looked from one to the other. "It's just kind of weird." Then she grinned. "But I can now afford to find a better office."

Reid laughed.

Brent held up some pages. "Got some stuff on that name you gave me Jac." He held out the papers. "There wasn't much to dig up." He frowned. "I don't get why a judge is ordering her to see Sandy, nothing turned up on a priors search."

She walked over and took the pages from him and began reading them.

She knew both men watched her as she paced across the room chewing her lip as she read through them. She looked up from one to the other. "That's weird. I don't know if Sandy should be dealing with this person."

Reid raised his eyebrows at her. "What are you going to do?"

She kicked off her shoes where she stood in the middle of the room while scanning the pages again. Mumbling under her breath, she walked over and sat in the chair pulling one leg up under her. Flipping the computer on she dropped her purse beside the chair and took off her jacket letting it drop onto the back of the chair. She didn't notice when it hit the floor instead. "Find out more." She said quietly more to herself then them.

Brent looked over at Reid and smirked.

Reid shook his head as he walked over and picked up the small-heeled shoes. Walking over, he bent down and put them on the floor beside the desk then picked up the jacket. Leaning over, he kissed the back of her neck. She only paused briefly to reach back and touch his cheek before she began typing again.

Brent handed him the morning report and picked up his cup. "I'll get coffee while you see what kind of fun we get to have today."

Reid studied the woman mumbling to herself quietly and grinned. Normally his mornings were ones that seemed dismal and mundane. Work wasn't such a bad place since his little mystic had walked through the door.

KEEP READING FOR AN EXCERPT OF

CAFÉ SERENITY

By Jacqueline Paige

1

"Remi. This *guy* wants to know what's on the bacon, egg and cheese bagel…"

Remi winced and dropped the paperwork she'd been struggling with. She looked out the kitchen window to see Iris, one of her waitresses, standing in the middle of the café surrounded by customers. Every single one of them now looking at her.

"Guess we don't need to ask how her hot date went this weekend," Darien mumbled from behind her.

Betany came running through the door and slid to a stop, her eyes wide. "She didn't."

Remi glanced above the door Betany stood in to see the yellow light was glowing. The light that let the staff and patrons know that there were *normals* in the café. Normals was the term they used to describe the completely vulnerable, none-the-wiser humans.

Betany waved her hands in Remi's direction. "Stay. I've got this." Taking a deep breath, a sweet smile appeared on her face as she stepped out into the customer area.

"Well," Berk cleared his throat and glanced from Darien to her. "Happy Monday morning." With that, he turned back to the grill and flipped the French toast.

"She's been doing so well," Remi whispered as she watched Betany smile and charm the customers.

Leaning his huge body on the counter beside her, Darien nodded. "Yeah, she hasn't stunned anyone in months."

158

It was only seven in the morning, too early for anything but coffee as far as Remi was concerned, never mind a faerie with an attitude. "I don't think she's cut out for mornings."

"No one in our world does mornings." Darien lifted her chin and forced her to look into his chocolate brown eyes. "You, for example, look like you haven't slept."

Sighing, she pulled away from his touch. "I didn't really. I'm trying to get all the paperwork caught up before that stupid audit." Glancing out into the dining area, she almost groaned in relief to see the customers Iris had embarrassed smiling and joking with Betany. Thankfully Iris was looking after another table, a stubborn set to her chin. "How can they be so different?"

Darien chuckled. "Just because they're the same race doesn't mean they have the same personality."

Picking up her cup, she sipped her now cold coffee while thinking about everything she had to do in the next few days.

"Hey," Darien leaned closer, "why don't you get Iris to give you a hand in the office?" He shrugged. "She's got one hell of a brain in her head, and with Nadine's little one teething and keeping her up all night I'm sure she won't mind covering the dining room and not having to worry about the extra responsibilities for a while."

Remi turned to see Iris heading to the counter, her small frame was rigid, her expression clearly said she wasn't in the mood for human *or* para interaction right now. "It would solve a few issues."

Darien hissed out a sigh of relief. "Whew. I was half afraid you were going to put her back on nights." He wiped his hand down the front of his black t-shirt, over muscles she tried not to stare at. "Then I'd have to deal with Pascal and Attis PMS-ing non-stop because they had to work with her again." He shrugged. "Everyone loves Iris, she's great to work with, if she's in a good mood, otherwise we're all terrified."

Remi doubted that Darien was afraid of anything. Rolling her eyes in his direction she smirked. "I didn't know vampires got PMS."

He grinned. "They don't, but they bitch like they do."

Glancing at the time, she picked up the papers. "Order has to be put away." She glanced at the stack of boxes in the backroom. "Are you sticking around for the meeting?"

Moving around her, he reached across the counter and picked

up the coffee pot and then grabbed her cup. Filling it, he handed it to her and smiled. "I've got the order and I'll do this morning's meeting, but I'll be late for this evenings." He winked at her. "If I don't grab a nap, I'll be grumpy tonight. We can't have a grumpy werewolf running Serenity After Dark." Giving her a heart-stopping grin, he sauntered out the door, grabbing a stack of boxes on his way past.

Remi watched the muscles flex in his arms and back as he lifted them with ease. Averting her eyes, she blew out a soft breath. Watching him made her flush all over her *whole* body. Turning, she noticed Berk was also watching Darien. He gave her a cheeky grin and then turned to serve up an order.

"It's not a crime to look," he wiggled his eyebrows up and down. "And I know better than to touch. I like all my appendages; attached and undamaged." He sighed dramatically. "It makes me sad though, so much man-meat and it's untouchable."

Shaking her head, Remi hugged the stack of papers into her chest and went over to lean at the end of the counter to wait for Iris to reach her.

Clipping her orders to the rack, Iris heaved a sigh and came to stand in front of her. "Sorry," she said in a somber voice. "They were so annoying asking about *every* single item on the menu. I mean if it says with cheese, they asked if it came with cheese…"

Remi could sympathize with her. Out-of-towners were so picky that way. "You could have passed them off to Betany, you know she doesn't mind."

Iris nodded, her short red hair bouncing with the motion. "I know. I just…" she sighed again.

"Listen," she gave her a hopeful smile. "I'd like you to help me get caught up in the office. With the auditors coming in two days, I need everything picture-perfect."

"Really?" Her eyes lit up.

"Yes."

She began untying her apron. "I'm all over that."

Remi looked over to where Betany was leaning, waiting for Berk to hand an order through the window. "Can you handle it for a few? Soren and the twins will be here shortly."

Betany nodded. "No problem, it's just coffee and a few orders right now."

Darien came back through the door and stopped to grin at the girls. "Disaster averted once again?"

Iris rolled her eyes and glared at him. "I wasn't going to harm them."

He chuckled. "Sure thing, Tink."

The ding of the door chime had all of them turning to see who came in. Back-up had arrived. Soren was moving quickly through the café in smooth graceful steps, like a cat, which made sense as she was a lynx shifter. Her smile was warm and friendly as she greeted the regular customers on her way past.

"Get Soren to help you if you get backed up before the girls get here." Remi told Betany as she motioned Iris to go down the hallway."

"I'll give them a hand." Darien added rubbing a reassuring hand down her back.

Remi smiled, even though she really wanted to step into his space and hug him. She'd be lost without him most days. "Thanks, Dare."

By nine thirty the breakfast customers were gone, a few regulars lingered watching the news channel while drinking their coffee. Most of them were retired or self-employed and didn't have to answer to the clock.

The elf twins, Ranae and Deanne were clearing tables and prepping for the next rush. Soren and Berk were in the kitchen preparing lunch items while singing show tunes. She didn't know how they did happy all the time, but it was better than working with grouches. Iris was content in the office entering data into the computer while Darien put the order away. Betany was helping him by restocking supplies. This left Remi time for some peace and quiet before more of the staff arrived for the meeting.,

Taking a stack of papers with her, she went outside to sit under the tree at the picnic table behind the café. It was silent out here for the moment, only a slight breeze was blowing; the sun was warm. The only sound was the gurgle of the water in the river as it moved downstream.

Flipping through the papers, she began to put them in order by date. Having to back-track into files that were five years old was an enormous task, and she was looking forward to it being done. Some of the papers in this pile went back as far as two years ago, when Doyle was still alive. She really needed to sort out the entire system he used to file and fix it.

Pausing, she looked up and stared toward the river. She still missed him. He'd been more of a father to her than any of the foster parents she'd had. Although, when she'd first met him, she thought he was insane or she might be having some sort of psychological break-down.

She'd been eighteen the first time she'd looked at the *Café Serenity* sign hanging out front, and the next seven years became a blur of edification that changed her life. Not just her life, but her mind-set and beliefs.

After leaving the foster system the second she turned eighteen, or as close as possible considering no one was one hundred percent sure of when she was born, she'd hopped on a bus with her starting-out allowance and ended up in Riverside.

On the bus she'd met a girl close to her age, Astrid. They'd hit it off right away. Astrid had invited her to stay with her, and even helped her get a job at the diner she worked at. Remi hadn't known a thing about waitressing, but with the customers demanding attention, she'd soon learned.

Things had gone well for about six months, until her life began spiraling downward, again.

Astrid's boyfriend, Carl, had tried to force himself on Remi. Thinking she was friends with her roommate had been Remi's first mistake. The second was telling Astrid about Carl, she freaked and kicked her out. Remi realized now she probably shouldn't have told her that he'd been screwing around on her for months with other girls.

Next thing Remi knew, she had no job or place to live. After sleeping in the post office for three nights, she'd gotten on the bus and headed to the other end of Riverside, setting out to find a place to live. Then she'd noticed the help wanted sign in the window of a unique-looking Café. Intrigued, she walked through the door. A café by day and a bar by night sounded interesting.

"Daydreaming?"

Remi jumped and turned to see Darien standing behind her, holding two plates.

"I brought you something to eat."

"Thanks." Setting her cup on the pages so the breeze wouldn't take them, she accepted the offered plate. "I was just thinking about Doyle," he handed her a fork, "about when I met him."

"You looked like a street rat when you came in." He took a bite of the hash browns.

"That's right; I forgot you were there that day." It was a lie; she could still remember seeing the large, muscular man unloading the delivery truck. She'd never seen someone with *that* much muscle up close before. Darien was one of those people that everyone looked at, it didn't matter whether you were a man or woman, you noticed him. He had soft understanding eyes, but his features were chiseled and hard, his body was too. All too often she'd overhear female customers calling him sexy and dangerous, in the same sentence.

He nodded slowly. "Yeah. I couldn't help wondering what Doyle was up to when he started showing you around without even knowing your name." He grinned. "Sneaky bugger that he was, placing a sign in the window only someone like *you* could see."

Remi took a few bites as she recalled. Doyle was a demon, what type she couldn't remember, there were far too many to know them all. A few days later when he sat her down and explained how he'd placed a sign in the window looking for her, and all about the para world, she'd thought he was crazy. He'd been seeking out an *almost human* to take in and train to run Serenity someday. Remi had never felt like everyone else, never quite fit in, but to be considered 'almost human', well even that was more than her off-center imagination could grasp. "You know I thought he was crazy when he told me I was almost human, but not quite."

Darien grinned. "You and me both. I thought he'd lost all sense bringing in a kid to mentor."

Pushing the plate away, she avoided the look he gave her, the one saying he wasn't happy she hadn't eaten all of it. "I was just grateful to have a place to live. I figured going along with his delusions wouldn't hurt anyone."

"Until your gifts started making an appearance…"

Stacking her half-eaten plate of food on top of his empty one, he leaned forward, his dark brown eyes moving over her face slowly.

"The first time you walked into Serenity After Dark and Pascal and Attis stopped and stared at you, I knew something was going on. I'd never seen them not be able to get inside someone's head."

Remi smiled. "Pascal is *still* trying to get inside my head."

He chuckled. "You'd think after seven years he'd give up."

Glancing down at the papers she frowned.

"You're really worried about this audit."

"I am. They're looking for something. The questions they asked were specific, not ones that you'd ask for in a random audit."

"You think someone pointed them in our direction?"

Nodding, she bit her lip. "How else would he know to examine the purchase orders?"

Darien reached across the table and squeezed her hand. "They're not going to find anything. Doyle's system keeps the unusual items in plain sight."

Closing her eyes, she exhaled slowly before looking back at him. "I hope so. Explaining bottled blood is not something even I could do."

"Remi."

Both turned to see Caitlyn leaning out the upstairs window. Caitlyn lived in the apartment at the back that Remi used to live in. She was nineteen and had been in Remi's care since she was thirteen, when her family had been killed.

Most days she was Remi's sunshine, that brightness in an otherwise dark world. Cait was a troll which, to Remi's mind before she met her, had meant big, ugly, fairy tale creature. The reality? Caitlyn was a petite, curvy beauty with snowy blonde hair, golden eyes and a smile that could thaw a glacier.

"I think you'd better come see this." She nodded to Darien. "Both of you." Her tone held a note of panic.

Remi glanced at Darien, his dark brows were drawn together in concern. Grabbing her cup and the papers, she got up and moved to the back door. She met them at the stairs, talking quickly and animated. Remi was only able to catch the main points, at least she hoped she did.

"So, Mel texted me telling me to check it out..."

Mel was one of Caitlyn's many admirers. He was a techie geek, a young werewolf that hung around whenever Cait was at work.

Cait practically danced on the spot as she turned her laptop around for them to see. Remi's stomach lurched as she looked at the gory pictures on the screen.

"Did Mel take these?" Darien asked his disapproval clear in his tone.

Cait gave him an annoyed look. "No. Mel would pass out if he'd seen this in person."

Reading the banner didn't help Remi understand. "Is this online for everyone to see?"

Cait tapped a polished nail on the screen. "No. It's only for our community, and you have to have a membership and password."

A glance at Darien's face told her this was news to him as well. Still confused, Remi looked away from the grizzly images of a shredded body to her charge. "So why are you showing us?"

Rolling her eyes, Cait leaned over the table and clicked on the screen. "Look." She enlarged photo.

Bending down, Remi focused on where she pointed. It was a picture of what was left of one blood covered arm, with a barely visible tattoo. Recognition had her straighten suddenly, her back bumping against Darien where he'd been looking over her shoulder.

"It's that inspector that was harassing us a few weeks ago." She tapped the screen. "He had this tattoo on his left arm. It's him."

Darien's hand rested on her hip as he stood close to Remi's back, the warmth from his higher body temperature didn't stop a shiver from going through her.

"Does it say what happened?" She swallowed and looked away from the screen to Cait.

Nodding, she brought up another page. "Word is he was ripped up like some crazed animal shredded him, but there's no bite marks to prove it."

"It's gruesome, honey, but what does that have to do with us?" Darien's breath brushed against the side of Remi's face, drawing her attention to the fact that he still stood close. Moving further away from him, she clutched the papers in her hand and shrugged at Cait.

Caitlyn gave a dramatic sigh. "He got all nasty and, in your face when you told him to take a hike."

Shaking her head, Remi glanced at Darien. "I didn't tell him to take a hike. I told him I had a business to run and couldn't have his minions getting in the way while they played with every wire and plug-in appliance."

"Still he was pissed and left saying he'd be back with a court order giving him the ability to do what he felt was necessary."

Darien rubbed the back of his neck. "We've scheduled the electrical updates. They'll be done in a few weeks."

Cait groaned. "They're going to look at *anyone* that had a problem with him."

"He was a pompous ass, Cait," Remi said quietly. "I'm sure a lot of others had a problem with him."

Sighing, she closed the laptop. "Okay, but don't say I didn't warn you." With that she flounced from the room, muttering under her breath.

Remi looked at the laptop.

"Hey don't worry; it has nothing to do with us." Darien's voice was soft and reassuring.

Remi glanced over her shoulder at him. "I hope you're right. With this audit I have more than I can handle."

Grinning, his eyes sparkling at her, he shrugged. "You don't give yourself enough credit, *Álainn*, you're stronger than anyone I know."

She hoped he was right.

KEEP READING FOR AN EXCERPT OF

The Huntress

Alterealm Series

Book 1

By J. Risk

Chapter One

I didn't even get both eyes opened and focused before I knew something was wrong. Where was the color? I was only seeing sepia? Everything was brown. Blinking rapidly, I tried to readjust my eyes to see if there was any other hue. It didn't change a thing and for the life of me I couldn't figure out why.

Sitting there, I tried to decipher what was going on and why I was sitting on the ground. Looking down I ran my hand over the dried dusty surface. Why was I on the ground? Craning my neck as far as I could in all directions, I looked around. Okay, where was the pavement and cement? The buildings and streets I called my natural turf?

The why's flying around in my brain suddenly decided the top question, was what the *hell* was going on?

Squeezing my eyes shut, I struggled to recall the last thing I remembered doing. I was hunting down a bounty—a nice one with a large dollar sign attached to her. I had tracked her ass down and...

I confronted her? Yes, I was minutes away from calling Frank and telling him to get out his shiny pen and sign my check.

So what happened between then and now? Not to sound repetitive, which is something that drives me nuts, but *what* the hell was going on?

Startled, I started to check for bullet holes or the deep crevices that knives leave behind in flesh. That had to be it, I'd taken a beating and this was that in between place you sit when your near death's door, but not quite ready to see what lies on the other side.

Finding no critical injury, I slumped forward and rubbed my head. There was some rational explanation for this, there had to be. Had I been drugged? It could be some crazy hallucination. Any minute now I was going to either wake up in my bed at home or some hospital with a cheery nurse leaning over me, reassuring me we are going to be *just* fine. I only had to wait it out a little longer and all would be normal.

To kill time until I woke up, I looked around some more. Wherever this was it looked like a burnt-out world. Not the charred kind of burn, but depleted and completely used up sort.

Vacant.

Sitting still wasn't really a strong trait of mine, so I figured I'd get up and take a look around, there had to be something to see around here. If my body was actually somewhere else for safekeeping, what harm could come to me, right?

I staggered like I'd never stood before, struggling to get my balance. Whatever was going on with me, my equilibrium was totally shot. Standing there swaying like grass in the breeze, I turned carefully trying to see if there was anything around me except rust tinted dirt and nothingness.

My heart stumbled around in my chest when I spotted someone coming in my direction. Yes! I wasn't the only one in this soulless place.

The closer it got to me made me the more I questioned my original conclusion. I didn't know, exactly, but it was not some*one* it was a some*thing.* No one label could describe it. Standing over six feet, it had the shape of a man dressed in jeans and a large, very out of fashion gingham snap up shirt. When I reached the face, I can only describe it as part wrinkle puppy dog with floppy skin crossed with Freddy and Jason after the slash scenes.

It stopped in front of me and instinct had me reach around behind me under my jean jacket for my raptor claw knife, which I put on as regular as underwear when dressing; and that would be everyday, by the way. Relief washed over me when I felt the small circular handle. At least while waiting to survive I got to bring my toys with me.

Big brown eyes assessed me slowly and I wanted to make the call that it was harmless, but yeah, having tracked down anything from a sicko killer to a card shark in the last three years, I knew better than to fall for sappy looks.

"Are you a magishian? You juisht appeared."

A male voice, even though he spoke with a heavy lisp that randomly inserted *ish* into his words. Then again if I had saggy lips like he did, I'd be happy to talk at all. I sized him up for a few more seconds, trying to gauge whether he was really in front of me, or if I was having some sort of psychotic episode. Was a magician good or bad? I decided the play dumb, being blonde did have *some* advantages. "A magician?"

Those brown eyes developed a nervous quiver. Magician equaled bad. "No…"

He looked relieved. "Oh good. I didn't want to have to bash you over the head."

I grasped my raptor tightly and shrugged. "Yeah, me either."

The sky brightened and began to glow a rust orange color. When I asked for some color, I'd hoped for something out of the orange family.

"We better go, they'll be coming soon."

"They?" I glanced around quickly, not wanting to take my eyes off him for long.

He nodded and pranced on the spot, the nervous movement had me on high alert. "The daywalkers." He whispered.

Daywalkers? Did I even want to know? I didn't think so, but this bizarre nightmare wasn't going to be complete if I didn't ask.

Looking me over a few times, his eyes widened under the pressure of his drooping forehead; *that* was quite the expression. "You're not one of them, are you?"

I walked in the day, night and even at dusk, but I wasn't going to tell him that. I decided honesty might work, if not violence was always a good backup. Judging by his expression daywalker ranked on the bad list with magician. "I—I don't know what you'd call me."

Those sappy eyes looked me up and down a few times trying to figure me out. "You better come with me. It's not safe to leave you wandering around." He looked behind him and then motioned behind me and started walking.

I knew in my gut it was a mistake, but as I had no other real options… I didn't know where I was or what was going on and so far he knew more than I did. "Where are we going?"

Pausing he glanced over his shoulder and then lumbered along again. "I'll take you to Troy, he'll know what to do."

My eyes were starting to strain as the sky brightened. "This Troy, he's in charge?"

He stopped so suddenly I almost ploughed right into his back. When he turned and looked at me, his eyes weren't a sad brown any more but were leaning more towards red. It had to be from the strange color of the sunrise. "You're not from Alterealm are you?"

"Is that where we are?"

He nodded.

"Nope."

That nervous jitter of his seemed to return all at one. "How did you get here?"

A reasonable question that I had nothing to offer that resembled an answer. "I don't know that either."

His red eyes darted to the sky. "We have to go."

Turning, he began jogging toward, well, nothing that I could see. Not wanting to find out what he was afraid of, I ran along behind him. All I could think was this Troy person, if he was a person, better have some answers.

He stopped again and dropped down onto his knees. Was he hurt? Surely that short jaunt hadn't winded him that much. He began tapping his hand on the ground. What was he doing? Looking all around us, I kept watch for anything really, not wanting to meet these daywalkers in the slightest. Just when I'd had about enough of his short break, he grasped something in the sand and pulled a door in the ground open.

"We're going to have to use the shortcut. We don't have time to get to the main gates."

Looking down into a hole with a ladder, I glanced around again and despite every muscle in my body telling me to run and get the hell out of here, I started down the metal rungs into a deep hole that would take me, hopefully back to friggin' reality.

172

HEART

Animal Senses Book 1

Jacqueline Paige

Chapter One

Blinking, Rayne glanced around. She was in the underground parking space in her apartment building and didn't even remember the drive. Her chest hurt, hands were vibrating and reality felt far away. Three times, she tried to extract the keys from the ignition, finally after fumbling she managed. *Come on, Rayne, get it together. Think!*

Her mind didn't want to accept the words that had come from Aiden's mouth, her fiancé. In all the years she'd known him, never had he used that tone. Scared her enough to send chills through her spine. She believed he meant every word. *I am not an idiot, I've always known he was a hard man, but the words turned my blood to ice and a part of me knows I'll never feel the same for him again.*

Taking a shaky breath, she groped around for her purse, feeling like she was moving through mud. Somehow, she managed to move and get out of the car. Her legs still felt like rubber, but she couldn't stay in the parking garage all day. Turning, she forced herself to move to the door.

What am I going to do? I can't marry a man like that. I'm not even sure if I can look at him now.

Stopping, she looked at the elevator door. Just the thought of stepping inside left her feeling suffocated and trapped. Hugging the purse again, she turned toward the stairwell. *Keep moving*—she had to.

Trapped, I am, aren't I? Trapped in a relationship. Just that one word showed her the next move. She had to get out of this relationship.

Aiden was not her dream man, if such a thing existed, but he had been comfortable.   Admitting that, she now accepted that the relationship was too comfortable to be real.

When she reached her third-floor apartment, she wasn't out of breath. But, as numb as she felt, she wasn't sure if she *was* breathing.   Maybe this was just a dream and she'd wake up any second now.   Giving herself a small reprieve, she let that thought marinate for a few seconds before reality came crashing back.

It took her two tries to get the key into the lock.   *What had his associate said just before my world darkened?*   *"We haven't found a body or any sign of him, Aiden."* Him, who?   A body?   *A body!*

As Rayne stepped inside her apartment the dreamlike veil lifted away, revealing reality.   *A reality I'm not sure how I can live with.*   She quickly locked the door, all three locks.   Not it would protect her, Aiden had keys.   Leaning back against the door she tried to calm down and think.

Aiden was some sort of mob, mafia...*whatever?*   Standing there she waited to feel her doubts were unsubstantiated, but it didn't happen.   Her fear *was* the truth.   This explained the dangerous looking misfits he had in his employ. They had never quite *fit* she thought. Aiden wasn't a boy scout—she knew that. He was a powerful man, as his father had been, but what kind of power was now very clear to her. Closing her eyes, Rayne held a trembling hand over her heart, it was still beating too heavily. *I can't look at him again. Ever.* This only meant one thing...

She looked around the pretty apartment for a moment, taking two steps towards the kitchen before stopping.   She had to leave, now.   Everything was *his*. *He* paid for everything in this apartment, she worked in *his* gallery.   Her whole world was controlled by *him*...

Moving in a slow circle, Rayne studied everything in sight.
Every. Single. Thing.
Bought by him, in one way or another.   Taking a deep breath, she tried to exhale slowly.   Failing, her breath huffed out in one loud whoosh.   There was no alternative, she had to get out of here.
Today.
Right now.
Kicking off her shoes, she bent down, scooped them up, and headed towards the bedroom.

Faster than she ever changed before, the skirt was stripped off and tossed on the bed. Barely having both legs in her jeans, Rayne began pulling open drawers and cabinets, dumping the contests all over the bed. All she really owned were clothes, her beloved camera, laptop and a few mementos to remind her of her parents. All of it was going in her car. A thought made her freeze as she held the empty drawer over the bed— her car was in *his* name. Dropping the drawer on the pile, Rayne sat on the bed, defeated. In the mirror, a frightened woman stared back. Seeing herself was enough to jolt her back into action. Giving the frail looking reflection a determined nod, she made a solid decision. To hell with him. She was taking the car. He hated it, called it girlie, and complained it wasn't comfortable. *The car is now mine.*

Forty-five minutes later Rayne surveyed the bedroom. There was nothing left that she wanted. Leaning down and picking up the last bag, she went to set it with the rest. "This is pathetic, Rayne Andrews. Your entire life fits in six cases and a couple of purses."

She walked through the apartment for the last time, working out how to get all of the cases downstairs to the car without causing suspicion, when the ring of her cell phone pierced the silence. She looked over at her purse, the ringtone was Aiden's. A few seconds after it stopped, the phone on the table began to ring. *Can I do this?* Taking a deep breath, "Buy some time," she whispered aloud just before answering it.

"Hello?"

"There you are. You didn't answer your cell."

He may be using that soft tone, but she now *knew* what he was. "Oh, I was taking the garbage to the garbage room." Her hand shook as she held the phone and prayed that her voice didn't give anything away.

"Where the hell is that girl I pay to do that?"

Just the way he said it made her tremble. "I-it's Wednesday, Aiden. She doesn't come in today."

"Right. Listen baby, I may be here awhile. Could be most of the night..."

"That's—fine. I was heading to the spa shortly." Closing her eyes, she waited to see if he questioned that.

"Do you want me to come by in the morning to pick you up?"

For what? "Pick me up?"

He chuckled. "We have a brunch with Donny and his wife."

Letting out the silent breath she'd been holding. "Oh, yes please." *Please let me sound normal.*

"Okay baby. You go get all beautiful for me and I'll see you in the morning. Ten o'clock."

"Okay, Aiden."

"Love ya, baby."

"Me too." She hung up quickly. Suddenly gasping for air, Rayne tried to settle her nerves again. *Ten o'clock.* Looking over at the clock and doing the math, she had seventeen hours to disappear.

It took almost as long to get all the bags down as it had for her to pack them. Of course, if you're planning to pack your whole life up and vanishing, it would probably be easier if you didn't drive a *Cabriolet.* Fitting everything into the micro-sized car had taken more than one attempt. In the time it took to finish, she was much calmer about her decision to leave. Not that she had a choice, but she could always have a mini breakdown and cry her heart out, later. Right now, she needed a plan to figure out the next step.

The first stop was the gas station. Getting out of the car, she looked around, checking for Aiden or one of his men. *Great, paranoia already.* After she assured herself that he couldn't possibly know yet, Rayne walked over to the pump. As she lifted the card up to the slot, she realized that he could track her cards. As if the machine was going to grab it, she jerked her hand back and turned to get her purse. She'd need all the cash she had available. Looking over her shoulder again, she walked to the cash machine. This location was close enough to the apartment to not point in any direction—when she finally decided on which direction. Her hands weren't the steadiest as she punched in the numbers and requested the limit the machine would allow, the shaking increased when she grabbed the cash and stuffed it in her wallet.

Glancing around, she walked back to the pump, inserting a card to pay for the gas. It only took her a few minutes to decide she would hit a few more cash machines in the area to bypass withdrawal limits. Aiden might not drive by, but now she suspected he had people everywhere that would recognize her.

After the gas was pumped, she thought that a map would be a good thing, unless she planned to drive around Chicago endlessly—because that's the only place she'd ever driven. Reaching down, Rayne pulled out the nearest one, only to put it right back, it was a map of the one place she knew. Bending down, she studied the title of each map before spotting an oversized atlas with Canada in it. She grabbed that one. Before she could second guess the decision, she set it on the counter and waited for the clerk to ring it in.

With the receipt and atlas clutched in her vibrating hand, she went back to the car, hoping she could get through the next few moments without questioning what she was going to do next.

An hour later, she sat in an empty parking lot, trying to force a bagel down her throat. The atlas she'd purchased was propped against the steering wheel, endless lines of varying colors stared back at her. So many places and no idea where to go. She looked over at the glove box where she'd put her money—in a make-up bag no less. It had taken five different bank machines to empty her accounts of every cent she had. Her cards were now at their limits, accounts were empty and on a whim, Rayne had taken out a cash advance on the card Aiden had given her for emergencies. If this wasn't considered an emergency, she didn't know what was.

Focus, Rayne. Looking back at the map, she tried to wash down a bite with the lukewarm coffee. She knew making maps took a lot of work and was complicated in a way she didn't really care to understand, but they really weren't telling her anything. She needed her laptop and the internet to make a decision that the squiggly color co-ordinated lines weren't telling her. Sighing, she glanced around the parking lot. A hotel was at the far end. She reached down to pull the laptop case off the floor. Setting it on the passenger's seat, she opened it and hit the power button, praying for it to pick up a signal as she flipped through another few pages. There was a signal, not a strong one, but it would do. Bringing up a mapping site, she entered Chicago as the starting point. *Now what?* A starting point generally meant you needed a destination and that she didn't have. Flipping a few more pages, Rayne picked the first name that jumped off the page. Destination? Timmins, Ontario, Canada. Her heart was pounding as she hit enter.

Strangely, she felt relieved knowing she had decided on a location. Her resolve only faltered for a few seconds when she discovered there was a fourteen-hour drive to get there. Biting her lip, she looked out the windshield, not really focusing on anything. Was she ready for a fourteen-hour drive that would take her far away from Aiden? If she had translated the map correctly, where she was heading was right in the middle of nowhere. That meant there was less chance of her being found. Yes, she was ready. Picking up the notebook that was waiting for the details of *the* game plan, she started to jot down the directions, deciding after a few lines that she'd only write down the first five hours and then reassess her route from that point. She had no idea what it was going to be like driving this far.

Closing the laptop, she put it back on the floor and just sat there. Was she crazy for doing this? Yes, but she couldn't stay here and that left few options. She was alone, just like when her parents died. This time all the decisions to be made were going to be her own.

~

Her eyes felt completely dried out. Was such a thing even possible? She didn't know, but at the first drug store, she was getting some eye drops. Glancing at the time— again, Rayne squinted back at the road. *How long have I been driving now?* Four hours? No, closer to five, she needed to stop soon. A few hours ago, she had foolishly thought she would be across the border before planning a stop, but that wasn't going to happen. Driving at this speed meant she still had at least an hour and a half to go before reaching Mackinaw City and then another hour to the border. Considering the longest she'd ever driven passed an hour back, Rayne knew she wasn't going to make it. She had a newfound respect for people that drove for a living. The quick bathroom stop a few hours before hadn't been long enough. If she didn't stop soon, she was going to make mistakes and end up lost, or worse. Stopping would be for the best.

Blinking quickly, she tried to make her eyes not feel as dry and then focused on the sign she was coming to. A motel was thirty miles from here. Looking at the speedometer, Rayne attempted to do the math and calculate how long that would take, less than a minute later she gave up and decided it wasn't important. As long as she arrived at the motel before falling asleep. A few hours of rest, something to eat and a shower became the new goal.

After what felt like ten hours she could see the hotel's sign not too far ahead. Elation and a bit of pride filled her as she realized she'd made it to here without help. She was slowing down when she noticed two police cars sitting at the motel. All the hair on the back of her neck stood up. Aiden couldn't know she was gone already, could he? Would he involve police? Biting down on her lip, she thought he probably wouldn't, but she wasn't going to take any chances. Gripping the steering wheel tighter, her heart was crashing against her ribs at the thought that Aiden might find her. There would be more motels further away, and another chance to take a break.

It took several seconds for the sign she'd just passed to register. *I've done it!* She was almost to Mackinaw, at least that's what the sign had said. Taking a deep breath and fighting the grogginess that had been closing in for hours, she forced herself to keep going. Maybe a little air would help, not that it had a half hour ago, but it couldn't hurt. She rolled the window down, hoping it would help. Seven hours of driving, minus two very brief bathroom breaks and a stop for gas, and she'd managed to keep going. If she wasn't ready to pass out, she would be pretty impressed with what she'd managed.

After a few minutes of taking deep breaths she groaned, the open window wasn't working. Reaching for the radio, she fumbled with the buttons and flicked through the few stations that were clear, anything to sing to or even pretending to sing might work. She scowled at the radio. Turning it off, she stared at the road once again. "Okay," she tried to ignore how slurred her voice sounded. "Use your brain, get the blood pumping and drive." Wiggling a bit, she tried to sit straighter. "Great, my brain is already sleeping," she yawned while trying to see the sign that was getting closer. "Oh. Interstate one twenty-seven. I've been looking at that for what seems like forever," she mumbled to the eyes in the mirror. "And before that it was I31." She bobbed her head and tried to recall the roads before that. "One ninety…something, not that it matters really—It's not like I'm going to be going on the return trip," Rayne snorted and then laughed, not sure if it was delirium or exhaustion that had her talking to herself. "And what are you going to do when you reach your middle of nowhere in Canada, Ms. Andrews?" She glanced at the speedometer, even though she had no idea what it had said on the Mackinaw sign she'd just driven past. Clearing her throat, she looked at the reflection again. "I have no idea what I'm going to do. I didn't sit down and plot out a course of action before fleeing," she giggled quietly this time and then squealed as she drove by another sign. "What–ah, miles..." biting her lip a couple of times, she looked at the time. "Oh! A half hour!" Gripping the steering wheel with the very last of her energy, she focused on the road. "You did it. And the reward?" She attempted to smile, but yawned and erased what would have been the smile. "The reward is sleep."

Rayne stood, clutching the room key in her hand and looking at the car, deciding. With the way she'd stuffed the cases into the car, there was no easy way to get to the one that had the clothes she wanted, without taking everything out of the car. Did she care if she slept in something fresh? At this point, no, she would come back out later and sort out what to change into. As she started to head for the room, her brain flashed a warning. She wasn't feeling very trusting now. Turning back, she unlocked the car and reached in to grab her purse, money, camera and laptop. If anyone decided to pick up the tiny car and carry it away, she could get by with just this.

Stumbling into the dark room, she kicked the door closed. Her shoes were off in two steps, it felt glorious. Her leg smacked into the bed. Setting the precious items down on it, she shoved them to the other side and flopped down, face first. Had she asked for a wakeup call? The chances of a yes were high, but there was no way she could summon the energy to find out.

About the Author

Jacqueline Paige lives in Ontario in a small town that's part of the popular Georgian Triangle area.

She began her writing career in 2006 and since her first published works in 2009 she hasn't stopped. Jacqueline describes her writing as *all things paranormal,* which she has proven is her niche with stories of witches, ghosts, psychics, and shifters now on the shelves.

When Jacqueline isn't lost in her writing, she spends time with her five children, most of whom are finally able to look after her instead of the other way around. Together they do random road trips, that usually end up with them lost, shopping trips where they push every button in the toy aisle, hiking when there's enough time to escape, and bizarre things like creating new daring recipes in the kitchen. She's a grandmother to nine (so far) and looks forward to corrupting many more in the years to come.

Jacqueline also writes under the pseudonym of J. Risk

Jacqueline loves to hear from her readers, you can find her at

http://jacquelinepaige.com/

Author note:

Did you enjoy reading one of my books?

If so, PLEASE help spread the word on social media. You can help by sharing on Facebook, tweet about it, post something on Instagram, Pinterest. Posting a review on your favorite book sites go a long way to help authors. With your help in keeping my books "out there", I can continue writing to keep those stories coming.

Writing and promoting can be very time consuming. I love talking to readers, but the hours spent on keeping so many social media outlets current can become overwhelming and time for writing pays the price. If you can take a few minutes to help, that would be awesome. Thank you!